By B. S. H. Garcia

The Heart of Quinaria

<u>Novels</u>
Of Thieves and Shadows
Of Love and Loss (forthcoming)

<u>Novelettes/Novellas</u>
From the Ashes*
From the Depths

*From the Ashes is free to my mailing list subscribers at
www.bshgarcia.com/subscribe

FROM THE

DEPTHS

THE HEART OF QUINARIA NOVELLA

B . S . H . GARCIA

First edition: February 2024

Cover design by MIBLART

Silhouette art by Jared Garcia

Interior design by B. S. H. Garcia

ISBN: 979-8-9867208-7-6 (hardback)
ISBN: 979-8-9867208-6-9 (paperback)
ISBN 979-8-9867208-5-2 (ebook)

www.bshgarcia.com

For Tyler, Ryan, and Mackensey.

Sorry I loaned you my books and charged you late fees no matter how early you returned them. We're even because you made me play Susan when we'd pretend to go to Narnia.

We all know I should've been Peter. I'm the oldest.

CONTENTS

No man chooses evil because it is evil; he only mistakes it for happiness, the good he seeks.

-Mary Wollstonecraft

KONAR

K onar ducked just as an object the size of his fist whizzed past the spot where his head had been. It slammed into the jointed, fibrous stalks of bugana that made up the siding of the hut he leaned against and fell to the ground in gleaming shards. Luminescent ink dripped down the siding and pooled beside the broken shell. He closed his book—an anonymous, long-dead scholar's musings on ancient Nyzar—with a soft *thump* and brought it protectively to his chest, fixing his younger setata with a stern gaze. She batted her long eyelashes at him as she danced a safe distance away. Amma had fastened Karliah's thick, white hair in multiple braids and piled it all atop her head, but the girl and the southern wind had played hard that morning, and a few curled strands tickled her forehead and cheeks.

"There are other ways to get my attention," Konar growled, kicking some hard packed sand over the shell. "Ones that don't risk damaging irreplaceable texts with permanent ink."

"You mean like shouting your name half a dozen times? Tried it." Karliah's eyes narrowed as her smile widened, an attempt to appear devious that was entirely negated by her slight frame and girlish features. She gestured to the beach a few yards away where a group of Az Zarian highborns clustered, pointing and gawking at a swarm of screeching seahawks as if the little scamps didn't frequent their own shoreline. "I'm about to give my best performance yet. Thought you might find it more interesting than reading about dead people."

"You thought wrong."

They glared at one another, gazes locked in a friendly rivalry common to siblings, their bodies close enough to reach out and touch, yet guarded enough that even their blood bond couldn't work its magic through the protective shells encasing their souls.

A recurring fear surfaced within Konar, one that whispered they'd always be this way, a barrier forever between them, growing, growing, yawning wider and wider until they could no longer see each other beyond the chasm. He blinked it away, letting it fall into the depths of his unconsciousness, and came to stand beside Karliah. He draped an arm across her shoulders, happy to let the feeling go as easily as it'd come.

Emotions were fleeting.

Konar arced his neck, placed a kiss on the top of her head. "But since you've robbed me of my increasingly rare pleasures, go on then. Showcase your budding awskada powers."

Karliah drank in the compliment as though it were the highest praise. And on the Islands of Zelos, it was. "In the time it takes Amma to prepare jellyshark stew, I'll have eighteen pieces of aspar. Maybe even a new scarf." A small sigh escaped her lips as she traced the frayed edges of the red silk tied around her neck.

It wasn't really a scarf. Scarcely enough material, and threadbare besides, but ever since she'd swiped it from an out-of-village patron at The Siren's Song a few moons back, it'd not left her neck. Konar gave it a playful tug. She slapped his hand away, equally playful.

"That's an oddly specific number of aspar," he mused.

"Six Az Zarian highborns. I figure I can get three a piece."

She spoke with such confidence that Konar had little reason to doubt her as she marched down the ghost of a path leading from the abandoned storage hut to the place where the sea grass and hardpacked sand gave way to curved waves of scalding grains fine as satin. At the base of a dune, she stopped to greet Chryia, a weathered old woman with a rickety cart filled with all sorts of random objects she pawned off on visitors—some of them rare, most of them not. She was a favorite target of Karliah's as she often took little dozes along the beach or in the village center, following patches of shade around and leaving the cart unattended long enough for small hands to slip into her goods unnoticed.

Konar followed Karliah to the edge of the beach, then positioned himself beneath the shade cast by the fanned leaves of a zidel tree, close enough to intervene, but hidden enough to stay unnoticed, which is how he planned to remain. Even at eight, Karliah rarely required assistance with such matters.

"Good sirs," she began, shouting from a distance. As she drew nearer to the highborns, her voice disappeared in the cacophony of waves and seahawk screeches.

Konar glanced down at the book, tracing his fingertip over the outlines of three moons seared into the leather cover. A common enough symbol in Quinaria, the moons did little to betray the author's identity, but Konar was almost certain the mystery writer was human. Something in the way they mentioned the passing of seasons over and over again, how they reminded the reader that the time to act was always *yesterday*, and if not yesterday, then today. And that life slipped through one's fingers faster than water through a fishing net. Having only lived through twelve of the five hundred or so years of his lifespan, the idea of the end was murky and distant to Konar. It carried no more bite than the fear of drowning when one's feet were secure on land.

Still, the author wrote with a sense of urgency that wormed its way deep into his mind, planting seeds of terror in his thoughts, haunting his everyday actions with questions of worth, of purpose. Of the meaning of it all. Thoughts no young man of an inconsequential future needed to worry himself with, or so his appa had said. Those were the parting words he'd spoken to Konar not a fortnight prior, before setting to sea. Their sting hadn't lessened with time, only festered and spread the way an infected wound did when it went untreated.

Sometimes wounds were beyond treatment. It wasn't unheard of to remove the entire affected area, be that a large patch of flesh or a gangrenous limb. It felt wrong to compare Appa to something so grotesque and worse to consider removing him from his realm of influence altogether, but Konar wasn't about to let a bitter man's resentment cloud his own bright future.

"'Words are our first weapon and our final hope,'" he whispered, quoting one of his favorite passages from the book. "'And no one can take them away.'"

A gust of wind ripped across the beach, slamming into Konar and forcing the book's cover open so the exposed pages danced and pulled at their binding. He slipped it back into his belt, promised not to take it out again until Karliah's little game was over, and directed his attention back to the Az Zarians gathered around his setata in a semi-circle like worshipers admiring a deity. Whatever lies she spun, this endeavor consisted of large swooping motions and the occasional flared hand to the forehead to imply something tragic. The highborns didn't try to stop her, nor did they continue their stroll down the beach. Reserved, albeit attentive, they stood uniformly, stiff as statues, arms crossed with hands hidden in swaths of vibrant silks, their hair cleanly cropped or gathered into sleek knots on the tops of their heads.

Konar didn't need to be within earshot to know what tales Karliah beguiled them with. It was likely some iteration of her usual:

Please, good sirs, spare me a moment of your time? I'm an orphan, you see. My parents died of the blue fever, leaving me and my little bretata all alone.

The little bretata part was her favorite. If Konar was close by when she said it, she'd sneak a devious glance in his direction.

Amma and Appa were followers of Mavet, she'd continue. *They spent all their free time volunteering at the mission, giving their money and resources to help further the teachings of our lord and savior. It is my wish to sail to Cadar and take my vows, for there is no greater honor as a woman than to be Mavet's bride.*

At this point, the Az Zarian highborns were typically entrenched in her story, filled with pity for her unfortunate circumstances, yet equally full of admiration for her steadfast desire to serve the religion they'd forced upon the Zelosi people. A religion whose teachings they happily abandoned when visiting Zelos to secure pleasures no longer available in their homeland.

And after they complimented her faith, told her what an example she was to her people, or something of the like, she'd open her eyes as wide as possible and drop the big request:

Please, oh faithful followers of the one true god, if Mavet so places the burden upon your hearts, consider sparing some aspar, that his humble servant might make her way to the promised land and better learn his teachings. Then I may return to my people with the proper knowledge to save their souls.

It was a good speech. Though it varied with each delivery, the message was the same. It'd grown the past year, with Karliah adding on convincing details and dramatic gestures as it suited her. She'd delivered it maybe fifty times and had at least three times the aspar to show for it. Some of that was due to her blossoming pickpocket skills, but for the most part, the highborns gave willingly, happy to help an innocent girl throw her life away in service to the lord they grew fat off.

"You thieving miscreant!"

A shriek cut through the roaring waves and sent prickles up Konar's arms. One of the highborns lurched for Karliah, grabbing her by the hair and yanking her back toward him. Konar's mouth went dry as he reached for the knife tucked into his knee-high boot, his sweaty, trembling fingers curling around the leather wrapped hilt. He'd never used it, never even needed to brandish it. Karliah never needed protecting, not with Appa around, not with her spidery reflexes and—

Another scream assaulted his ears.

Karliah had scrambled away from her captor and into the arms of another. They closed in on her like the packs of wild dogs that wandered the streets of Tongura at sundown, looking for scraps of food or poultry escaped from makeshift pens.

Konar emerged from his hiding place, his knife held before him like a shield, sand making his strides awkward and uncertain. The burning sensation in his lungs and the way his grip on his knife loosened with sweat only further weakened his confidence.

And how do your words serve you now, young scholar? Appa's voice echoed through Konar's mind with words that had never been spoken aloud, yet carried no less weight.

Words are weapons, weapons are words, he answered, this time in his own voice. He'd use both—all, everything—to save his setata.

When Konar was twenty feet away, one of the highborns noticed him advancing and hastily yanked the excessive sleeve draping off his comrade's arm. Two pairs of eyes locked onto him, then another. Konar forced his legs forward despite their unwillingness to comply. The sun shone unhindered overhead, dazzling the green-blue waters in ironic splendor, the seahawks, the crabs, the fishing boats yards out from the shore, all oblivious to his predicament.

Ragged breaths scraped against his lungs. He'd reach the highborns in moments, and then what? They were all nyrian, like Konar, and at least two of them had not yet let their luscious trappings weaken their physicality. He flicked through options like pages in a book, racing through them faster and faster, fearing more with each moment that there wasn't a good way out of this. Shout at them? Fight them? Stab as many of the rich bastards as he could and hope Karliah would flee in the chaos?

Oh, First Amma, he was going to die. If not now, then surely when word got out that he'd spilled highborn blood.

A tear slithered down his cheek as he directed the knife to the nearest highborn's throat, only feet away now, the man's beady eyes wide with the reality of his fate, shocked at the audacity of a lowly pirate whelp like Konar daring to take his life.

Then, Konar wanted to do it, just for a moment. He actually wanted to take his lyvium blade and plunge it between the highborn's neck rolls.

And that was what stilled his hand.

A sick sensation swarmed in his stomach, like eels writhing in nets on the docks, their snake-like bodies cold and hateful as they convulsed helplessly toward a sea they'd never again inhabit. The highborn's eyes transitioned from fear to hatred, and he smacked Konar's hand, knocking the blade into the sand. They looked at the knife, then at each other.

"You bitch!" a voice rang out.

Konar glanced up, caught a glimpse of Karliah sprinting away from her captor, the man now holding one hand limply and peering closely at his flesh as though he'd been bitten by a rabid beast.

Karliah flailed a beckoning arm as she fled. "Run, Konar! Run!"

A loud *smack* sounded in his ear, accompanied by a sharp sting. Konar stumbled back, falling butt-first into the sand. The highborn towered over him, deep set lines pulling hard at the edges of his eyes. Slowly, his hand curled into a fist.

Konar shut his eyes to brace himself for pain, but the scowling face of Appa filled his mind, obscuring all other fears. He lurched for the blade blindly, dodging the highborn's swing. He tried to sprint away, but hands latched onto his ankle and flattened him back on the sand, face first. Konar rolled onto his back and threw fist after fist, his attempts hesitant and defensive. More hands clamped around his wrists, then one around his other ankle, his last free limb. A scream clawed at the back of his throat as he struggled to pull free from the ever-tightening grips. His chest heaved, slick with sweat. Even if the Az Zarians didn't kill him, Appa would, for losing this easily, for leaving Karliah unprotected in the first place.

I'll show you, Konar told the figment of his appa.

Using the sweat he'd worked up to his advantage, he managed to slip one hand free and drive it into a highborn's ear. He swung again, but before his fist made contact, his next target fell back, moaning and clutching his head. Blood seeped between the man's fingers. Beside him, the blood-stained shell of a spined oyster lay in the sand, as if it had always been there.

But that kind of shell wasn't native to this beach.

Konar blinked, his mind a torrent of panic working against his memory. Chryia's cart. It was just beyond the slope of the dune and filled with all kinds of oddities.

Karliah had come prepared. She'd lingered nearby, even after her narrow escape, risking her life to give Konar a fighting chance. And now, it was his turn to save her.

Konar leaped for his knife with swift confidence as a figure approached in his peripheral. He snagged it a moment before the highborn sunk thick fingers into the sand where it had lain. Eyes filled with vengeful hatred sought his own. The highborn's lips pulled back in a snarl.

"Don't you dare—"

Konar kicked him in the mouth. Hard. Blood trickled over the highborn's thin lips, staining his silver skin red. He hunched over, pawing at his face and cursing as his uninjured companions rushed to his aid.

Nausea surged through Konar's stomach. He scrambled to his feet and raced down the beach, first by instinct alone, then slowly, slowly drawing other senses back into his control. The wind slipped into the open collar of his loose-fitting shirt, offering him a taste of relief. His pace slowed enough for him to pick out the finer details of the sand.

There. Footprints. Tiny and faint, leading toward a break in the thick growth of the jungle.

Voices grew louder behind him. Closer.

Konar sprinted as fast as his legs would allow. He pushed until his lungs burned, then pushed beyond that. Sand flew behind him like ocean spray. The voices softened and dissipated into the crashing of waves as he slipped between trees, smiling a little as the carpet of fallen branches and leaves gave his feet wings.

He knew where she'd be, and they'd never catch him. Not in his jungle.

Konar peered out from his shelter of ferns, his senses attuned to the sights and sounds around him. Ahead, a mist hovered above the surface of a pool where a waterfall fell to the basin, its texture caught somewhere between sea foam and mist. Smooth-faced rocks smattered with bulges framed the hide-away that lay beyond the waterfall's veil, and above them tow-ered trees with feather-shaped leaves as teal as the water and as large as Konar's arm span. Birds shrieked from the tops of branches, breaking up the steady monotone of buzzes and clicks from the countless insects populating the foliage. Unless something had happened, Karliah would be hidden behind the waterfall, tucked into the shadows of the grotto.

Satisfied there was no imminent danger, Konar ventured out from the ferns. A cool breeze lifted off the face of the water and washed over him like a fog. He walked to the edge of the pool, ready to strip his clothes and plunge into the transparent water. Instead, he settled for scooping some up with his cupped hands and bringing it to his face, splashing it over his neck, his hair, and finally quenching his thirst with the water many in the village believed to be sacred. He wouldn't rejoin Karliah until he was certain of his anonymity.

A hiss sounded from the ferns behind him. Two fiery eyes appeared, then a serrated beak with overlapping teeth. The creature they belonged to scarcely reached the mid-way point on Konar's calf, but that did little to dampen its lust for blood.

Konar retrieved a smooth stone from a shallow spot in the pool and hurled it into the ferns masking the creature. With leaves the size of a grown man, the ferns only offered a slight shiver in response to the intrusion of the rock, but the creature shrouded beneath them made a guttural shriek and skittered back into the jungle.

Convinced he'd not been followed, Konar tucked his boots beneath the ferns and dove into the water, shivering at the sudden change in temperature. Karliah needed him, and he didn't want to wait around for the gwanei to notify its pack. Alone, the carnivorous little reptile could only do so much damage on two legs with an arm's reach no longer than his hand. But together, in their swarms of thirty to fifty, their razor beaks and toothed tongues could strip even the largest of creatures down to the bone in a matter of hours. Just the other day, he'd witnessed them making quick work of a beached sea cow. He'd dared a little nearer than normal, hoping to get close enough to the sea cow carcass to take some notes and make a sketch in his journal. That lasted all of five minutes. Then the pack had turned on him, fangs and claws thrashing with speedy legs that nearly overtook his own lung-bursting sprint.

Never again. That was not the life he desired. No beasts, no brawls, and no battles.

Konar emerged on the other side of the waterfall and drew the first truly relaxed breath he'd taken since the incident. Sunlight filtered into the grotto, reflecting the ripple patterning of the water onto Karliah's glistening cheeks.

A pang struck his chest. He pulled himself onto the slick rocks and drew her to him in a silent embrace.

"I thought they had you," she whispered into his chest as he stroked her back. "One of them had a large pouch tied with a thin leather cord to his belt. I thought I could cut it quickly with my knife and steal more aspar than I bet you I could. I didn't mean to..."

A sob choked off the rest of her words. Konar hummed in response, a melancholy tune his amma had used to soothe them both to sleep as babes, and still occasionally did, when something ailed them. A song of the First Amma and the child she created out of love and her own flesh, a child who, after departing the paradise of her womb, died instantly.

For the world is a cruel place, Amma would say after singing in the ancient speech of the awskada. *But she gave that child a kiss of life, pouring her heart and soul into the babe, and where there had been death, there was life. And this is why there is no kiss as powerful as an amma's, nor a love as pure.*

Karliah pulled away. Wiped the tears from her eyes. Then she reached into her vest with a coy smile and pulled out a pouch that she dumped on one of the flatter rocks. The clinking of aspar echoed throughout the cave. At least three dozen pieces, some larger in size and therefore value, lay at their feet.

"I don't know if I should be proud or angry," Konar said, biting back a smile.

"You sound like Appa." Karliah rolled her eyes as she picked the coins up one by one and placed them back in the pouch. "You can be both, though. Just don't tell Amma." She glanced side-eyed at him. "Promise?"

Konar shook his head. "I'll only promise if *you* promise to never do something like that again." He offered her his pinky finger. "Deal?"

Karliah let out an exasperated sigh as she fastened the pouch to her belt. "Deal." She extended her pinky toward his, stopping just shy of touching it. "But you also have to promise you'll never, ever leave me. Otherwise, I might be tempted to do something—how does Appa say it? Rash?"

"Rash, yes. It means—"

"I understand what it means." She intertwined her pinky with his. "I promise," she whispered.

That ghost of a fear resurfaced in Konar's mind, whispering of unkept promises and broken hearts. He chased it back into oblivion.

"I promise, too, Setata," he whispered back. "I swear it by the First Amma, and the Last."

KARLIAH

K arliah emerged from the jungle and made quick work of inspecting the clearing surrounding the Brune family hut. It'd been hours since her near-deadly pilfering at the beach, and though the round-bellied silkies had no reason to know who she was or where she lived, Appa said one could never be too sure in such situations.

She checked the perimeter first, as he'd taught her, then moved in to inspect the more subtle details. Not that she knew exactly what to look for, other than the obvious: blood or bodies. Thankfully, neither tarnished the landscape, and the hut was as she had left it that morning. And—she inhaled deeply—there was the scent of Amma's cooking. Wild hog, from the smell of it. Her stomach growled in response, and she sprinted toward the stairs, leaping over the ring of ferns that surrounded their territory like a natural fence.

Like most Zelosi dwellings, the Brune hut was elevated several feet off the ground in case of flooding or beasts of ill intent. Appa and Amma had built it themselves, long before she was born, and other than their ship, *The Umbra*, it was their pride and joy. Two levels, imported sun-blood wood from Az Zar, beautifully carved gables reflecting the lifecycles of the moons, and a wrap-around deck with a simple, yet quality, waist-high railing. Karliah loved that part the best, loved to soak in the tepid night air, swinging her legs in a gentle rhythm while the sirens serenaded her with their eerie melodies.

Eerie in a good way.

They sounded as though they'd lived a thousand lives and lost a thousand loves. At least, she liked to think so. On rare evenings, she might glimpse one flying past, its shimmering, midnight-blue feathers catching the moonlight.

Karliah stopped at the top of the stairs and peered over her shoulder. Konar followed, but he walked as slowly as a fly in a syrup trap. Inside, Appa's and Amma's voices carried beyond the walls, spiked with tension but still lowered enough that she couldn't make out what they argued about. She sat on the top step and gave Konar her best hurry-up glare. She wasn't going in without him.

"Did you age two hundred years on the hike back?" she said when he joined her. "I'm starving."

He looked from her to the door and rubbed his face in the exasperated way grown-ups often did. "What are they going on about this time?"

Karliah shrugged and eyed the door. "You first."

"You're the one they never get angry with." Konar reached for the handle, but Karliah grabbed his arm before he yanked it open.

"Remember, don't tell them about today. Not what really happened, at least. Promise?"

Konar nodded and held a finger to his lips.

The door swung open, nearly knocking her bretata down the stairs. He gripped the railing, wide-eyed and nostrils flared, as Korandon 'the Brineheart' Brune walked onto the porch with long, heavy-footed strides. Appa's pirate alias was the mainstay of his pride, a name given to him by his own appa who claimed his son was so in harmony with the sea that his heart pumped brine instead of blood.

One day, I'll have a special name, too, Karliah thought as Appa examined her and Konar with an air of suspicion.

He was more the Brineheart this evening than Appa, clad in his knee-length leather coat with a raised collar and lyvium buttons he'd fashioned from melting down plunder from one of his raids. His tricorn hat was pulled down far over his forehead, not that he had any wrinkles to hide, and his violet eyes shone extra bright, the way they did when he was up to something others might deem unlawful. Eyes that narrowed as they regarded her bretata.

"Straighten up then, boy," he said to Konar. "And don't act like you weren't eavesdropping."

Konar's lips parted. No words came out. Appa flicked his gaze to Karliah, and Konar slunk past him and into the hut.

"What's this?" Appa touched Karliah's cheek, tracing his calloused thumb over a spot that stung beneath his touch.

"Running through the jungle, Appa." She placed her hand on his and smiled.

"You, who's formed a kinship with the trees, who could find her way home blindfolded no matter where I drop her, who hunts poisonous snakes for fun?" He smoothed his mustache—not that it needed smoothing—and twisted the ends thoughtfully before stroking his beard in a similar fashion. "You will tell me the truth before the night's end, but for now, come. Your amma's prepared abdano."

Karliah's mouth watered, her fear of Appa learning the truth temporarily diminished by the thought of a good meal. After depositing a peck on his cheek, right on top of his scar—a wound he'd yet to tell her the story behind—she scurried inside.

The spicy and sweet notes of pyanne nearly overpowered the savory aroma rising from the piglet. Amma roasted it on a spit over the fire, turning it slowly and applying what appeared to be an endless supply of a bugana-based marinade. Konar bent over the prep table beside her, happily chopping away at some terredon, an aromatic root they both swore the meal would be incomplete without. A cup rested on the prep table, close to Amma. Karliah didn't need to smell it to assume its contents. She walked over to them, playfully bumping into Konar before wrapping her arms around Amma's waist from behind.

"Smells delicious," she said, wrinkling her nose at the stench of alcohol emanating from Amma. Karliah tried to inhale the meal and only the meal, but she was far too close to ignore Amma's perfume of choice.

Amma scratched beneath her eyepatch before taking Karliah's face in her hands and planting a kiss on her forehead. "I was going to make your favorite tonight, but Oska offered your appa a hog in exchange for the aspar she owed us, and being the generous man he is, he couldn't refuse."

Konar and Karliah exchanged glances as Appa gently shut the door behind him and took a seat at the table. He kicked his boots up and lit his pipe. Amma muttered something indiscernible under her breath, but Karliah understood well enough. It wasn't the first time Appa had let payments slide on his loans to pretty women, nor would it be the last.

"Oi, your boots, girl." Amma scowled, holding her at arm's length. "How many times have I told you to wipe that jungle filth off before coming in? Or better yet, leave them outside?"

Karliah cast a cautious glance over her shoulder to inspect the damage. She hadn't trailed in *that* much mud on the woven floor mats. Not as much as sometimes, anyway. But Amma wasn't worth arguing with on a sober day, much less now after who knew how many cups of kolaash and amid an argument with Appa.

A retort tingled on Karliah's tongue, and it took every bit of her resolve to hold it back. The instability Amma caused in their home made Karliah want to run away, to carve out a life that she controlled, and there had been several nights she'd done just that. Yet she always came back. She couldn't upset Appa, couldn't give Amma even more cause to scold her and treat her like an overgrown babe incapable of controlling her own bladder. Most of all, she couldn't do that to Konar. They always had each other to get through whatever strife Amma and Appa brought into their lives, and she wouldn't be the one to break that bond.

"Sorry, Amma." Karliah peeled the boots off and tiptoed back to the door, cracking it enough to toss the offenders outside before slinking to the table, where she took a seat beside Appa. "I'll clean up the mess after we eat. Promise."

Amma flapped her hands as if she was shooing a fly. "Bah, you and your promises, Karliah. Sometimes it's better to just do, yes?" She removed the hog from the spit and placed it on the prep table for Konar to plate, drained her cup and, apparently done with the pretense of moderation, grabbed the kolaash bottle and sauntered to her seat with it, her moon-patterned skirt swishing about her bare feet.

Appa's eyes narrowed momentarily before he tossed his hat onto the bed he rarely slept in. His absence was, in part, due to his frequent travels. Even Amma was only home half the time, and Konar and Karliah just a little more than her, when the missions were too high risk, or the hired crew unsavory. Still, Appa preferred to spend his land-locked nights in the company of friendly strangers or, even more often, alone. Poring over his maps. Smoking his pipe. Watching the stars. He said the moons wouldn't let him sleep, but Karliah wondered if it didn't have something to do with his conscience.

The Brunes looked everywhere but at each other as Konar approached from the prep table carrying a bugana-carved platter filled with the entirety of the piglet, along with pyanne slices as a garnish. He placed it in the middle of the table with a precision Karliah only dreamed of having and cleared his throat. Karliah shifted in her chair, wanting to dig in but not daring to do so until her parents partook. Whatever dark cloud hung between them was worse than Appa's infidelity or Amma's drinking, and she had a queasy feeling they were both one wrong action or word away from losing their controlled demeanors.

"Can I serve you first, Appa?" Konar asked, his voice cracking.

"I don't know, Konar." Appa didn't even glance at him. His unrelenting gaze was anchored to Amma. "Can he, Zorah? I don't dare make a decision without you."

"I'm not one of your whores, Korandon," she replied coolly. "Therefore, I have absolutely no tolerance for any more of your lies."

Appa took a long pull from his pipe. "Lies?"

He baited Amma with his blatantly exaggerated confusion, dangling it before her like the string Karliah used to entice the street cat that had lurked about their porch back when they lived in the village. It was one of her earliest memories, teasing the cat, watching its pupils narrow and its haunches shift as it burned with anticipation. Then it would leap, claws extended.

Amma leaped, just as the cat, and planted both hands firmly on the table with enough force to jostle her bottle. "I don't remember the last time you consulted me. Not on matters of business, family, or pleasure."

Karliah winced. There was no saving the evening now. They never came back from such arguments. It would take a few days (and bottles) for their anger to fade from bonfire to coals, and without the cause of the fight being addressed, there would only be peace for a time before one of them set it aflame again. Part of Karliah thought they actually enjoyed fighting. It was as if they got some sort of sick pleasure from it, the same way a child might provoke a snake with a stick, happy to go on disturbing its peace again and again, no matter the risk.

Konar cleared his throat as he reached for the piglet. "Amma, pass me your plate. I'll—"

Appa and Amma both started shouting at once, drowning out Konar's peace offering in a storm of angry accusations.

"—if you'd just trust me for once—"

"—you never consider me and the children—"

"—nothing makes you happy—"

"—I'm tired of this lifestyle, living in fear of the fallout of your choices—"

"—then leave, and let me handle—"

"—you'd like that, wouldn't you—"

Karliah felt herself shrinking, compressed, like a mud pie packed over and over again until it was as dense as a rock. A loud buzz sounded in her ears. Her body stiffened, jaw throbbing, stomach clenching, hands curling into tiny fists.

And then she screamed.

The expressions on Amma's and Appa's faces were identical: wide eyes, wide nostrils, and wide mouths, as if they were caught off guard, entirely unaware their offspring listened in on their newly aired grievances. Konar kept his gaze down, but the slight cock of his chin betrayed his curiosity at Karliah's sudden outburst, at the emotion she usually tried to control to appear older. He squeezed her hand beneath the table.

"Sorry, Karliah," Amma said. A soothing tone crept back into her voice, maybe intentionally—more likely instinctually. "You and your bretata shouldn't be forced to overhear such things."

"And why not?" Appa's voice had also regained some control, though there was nothing soothing about it. "Perhaps they should contribute to the discussion, as we can't seem to find common ground." He grabbed the carving knife from Konar and began slicing pieces off the piglet in tight, overly controlled motions. His compass necklace freed itself from the opening in his shirt and swung dangerously close to the knife. "What do you say, bounty of my loins? Would you like to settle this argument for us?"

"Yes," Karliah pleaded before Konar could object. "Whatever makes you two stop ruining the evening."

A dark, frightening chuckle emerged from Appa's throat. "Careful, or that confidence will be your undoing, young one." He sat back in his chair and took another pull from his pipe, leaving the sliced bits of meat untouched in the center of the table. "Alright, Karliah. What if I told you I'd been offered a job, one exceedingly difficult and dangerous that, if completed, could be the last job we ever take?"

"I'd be suspicious," she answered honestly. Appa always warned her to keep things to herself, but talking it through made the thoughts clearer in her head. "Do you even know how much we'd need in payment for it to be the last job we ever take? Would that much aspar even fit in our hut?"

A warmer, more genuine laugh escaped Appa this time. "Ah, my little siren, with this reward, we could buy our own island."

Karliah squeezed her eyes shut and tried to imagine what their island might look like, but before she could get beyond a private hut just for her, complete with her own deck and an entire level to practice swordplay, Konar sucked in a loud breath.

"How dangerous is it?" her bretata asked. "If the pay is better than we ever dreamed of, then the job must be near impossible, one we're likely to lose part of the crew attempting. And even if we don't fail, the person who hired you probably lied about the payment because no one has the means to offer us that much aspar, no matter your reputation." Karliah sensed him trying to make his voice deeper than it was, but it came out in a rushed, single breath, tainted with the cracks of a boy on the cusp of manhood.

"You're asking all the wrong questions, lad." Appa slipped a dagger out from the sheath on his belt and stabbed a piece of meat, studying it briefly before popping it into his mouth, where he chewed with fervor.

Outside, the first siren of the evening began a solitary lullaby. Amma nursed her bottle, her gaze foggy and distant as she joined in the ghostly tune with a complementing harmony. A grumble murmured in Karliah's stomach, but she couldn't eat until the matter was resolved. *Who,* she wanted to scream at Konar. *Appa wants you to ask who offered him the job.* She nudged his foot with hers, willing the answer to make itself known to him.

The message was lost on Konar. For all his books, he always seemed to run short of words with Appa.

"Everything I say is wrong," he muttered.

"*Who* is what's important, right, Appa?" Karliah asked, unwilling to wait any longer. And by answering yet another question aloud, further understanding struck her like the dawn. "Whoever wants to hire you isn't someone you can just say no to."

"There's a clever girl." Appa stabbed another piece of meat, but this one he placed on Karliah's plate with an approving grin.

Amma stopped humming. "He doesn't own us, Kor. Zelos isn't even rightfully under his control. He can't—"

"You think I'd work again if I refused him?" Appa jammed his dagger into the piglet's head. The table trembled beneath the force and knocked Amma's bottle onto its side. "This isn't an offer he's gone public with to secure the lowest bidder. It's something he wants done discreetly, and that's why he sought after me." He jabbed his chest with his thumb. "If I refuse, someone else will do it, *and* he'll put a price on my head."

"The emperor of Az Zar," Konar said, coming to the realization at the same time as Karliah. "What could he possibly want that he doesn't already have?"

Appa didn't look up as Amma stumbled out of the room, unlikely to return to them that night. "Now, you're asking the right questions. And I think the *what* might be something of interest to you."

"What in the name of the First Amma are you going on about, Brineheart?" Barky shouted.

Even seated an arm's length away from the man, it was hard to hear his bellow over the noise of the inn, a pleasant medley of musicians playing knee-slapping tunes on stringed instruments mixed with the kolaash-infused guffaws of the patrons. Someone shrieked, and, at least to Karliah, it was hard to tell if it was a pleasant sort of sound, the ones adults made the rare times they allowed themselves to play as children did, or an actual distress signal.

She decided it was the former. After all, she'd only had good experiences at The Siren's Song the half a dozen or so times Appa dragged her along on business. She loved all its chaos and constant commotion, all the brightly patterned skirts, frilled blouses, and clinking boots, the way the air buzzed with life, the familiarity of the regulars and the intrigue of the newcomers. She loved how, despite all the doors and shutters being propped open, the sticky air from the outside did little to alleviate the stickiness within, and how it smelled of sweet and spiced drink, of musky smoke and sweat. But most of all, she loved that she was simply allowed to be there, present with her appa in a place children so infrequently visited. Well enough liked, she might add, to get hugs from the serving wenches, a mug of pyanne juice from the innkeep, and a complimentary serving of Barky's famous fried kelp.

Barky flashed a gap-toothed smile as Karliah bit into an exceptionally crispy piece, and then the sun-weathered old human leaned across the table, plopping his elbows in a sticky puddle of drink that had likely been left to congeal for days. "Say it again," he repeated, fixing Appa with a squint-eyed gaze.

Appa sipped his pyanne juice, and Karliah almost giggled at the thought of the most fearsome man in the inn drinking a beverage most often consumed by children. But Appa had long since given up drinking. Weakened the mind and memory, he said. It was for youth and people with little ambition.

For people like Amma, Karliah thought, then she slumped in the booth as a wave of shame washed over her. Amma wasn't as bad as half the people present in The Siren's Song any given night, and was Appa's reliance on his pipe any better? It wasn't her place to judge, not yet. Not until she knew first-hand of the grown-ups' guilty pleasures and the days they toiled through to earn their respite.

"You, me, *The Umbra,* and maybe thirty or so sailors we've worked with in the past who can hold their tongues," Appa said, not once looking up from his drink.

Karliah noted that he didn't bother to use the word *trustworthy* to describe his ideal crew, and she figured it was intentional. Who, in Appa and Amma's line of work, could ever be trusted? She tucked the nugget of wisdom away. It was probably wise to apply that logic to everyone she crossed paths with. As long as she had her family, she didn't need to trust anyone else, anyway.

"I understood that part well enough," Barky grumbled. He gathered a loose bunch of his stained apron and used it to dab the sheen of sweat building up on his forehead. "But you're gonna need to elaborate on the religious artifact and vengeful benefactor bits."

Appa stuck out a strong hand twice the size of Karliah's. His sleeve was rolled up to his elbow, exposing a muscled forearm tattooed with the silhouette of an arzok. The dark, winged figure imprinted there with elongated ears and a tapering tail might have been Appa's kindred beast, and it might have been any number of the night demons (as they were often called) native to Zelos, lurking deep within caves of the ancient forests. One day, Karliah would have one, as her appa's family always had, and even though it was forbidden to give them names, she liked to think she'd be the first one to have a close enough bond to do so.

Barky took a swig from his mug—most certainly alcoholic—as he eyed Appa's hand. "So it's like that, is it? Even with your oldest friend?"

"Especially with my oldest friend."

A groan escaped the cook's lips. He raised his hand, signaling one of the attending wenches to his side, then slipped a coin in her low-cut blouse as she refilled his mug. Appa leaned back in the booth, one arm draped over the wave-patterned backrest, the other drawing his pipe from his overcoat.

"Fine," Barky muttered after he'd worked his way through half his refill in record time. He gripped Appa's outstretched hand. "You know I can't refuse promises of riches, and at this age, what do I have to lose? I only keep this job for the in-between. And the company." He winked at a busty woman in a black fitted halter as she walked by, earning himself little more than an eye roll. "But while Jezkaab was a fair employer, his son's a downright brownnosing little shite. And the cooking grows tiresome, so it does."

Appa nodded, his full lips drawn into thin, hard lines. He poured some ground leaves into his pipe and lit it, offering it to Barky before partaking himself. The cook leaned his thick neck over the table and smoked directly from Appa's hand, his own hands wrapped tightly around his drink. An unspoken agreement passed between them, one drawing on experiences that long predated Karliah's meager existence, one that could never be measured by verbal promises. Appa smoked after Barky, and then it was done. The buzz of the inn seemed to fade, as if paying respect to the agreement entered into by two men who'd known each other for half a human lifetime.

"What've you anchored me to this time, Kor?" Barky asked. He dug into the bitten nail of his thumb with his forefinger, his brown eyes as fierce as any nyrian's, despite the lack of luminescence. "What sacred artifact is in question? I never took you for a religious man."

"The gods and goddesses exist," Appa said, his tone sincere. "It's our ideas of them that need reckoning. But that is neither here nor there. This artifact, as you put it, could also be considered academic in nature. We won't know until we find it. Assuming it exists."

"Few zealous dreamers could convince you to go on chasing their ghosts with very little to go on, but it sounds like that's exactly what you signed up for." Barky leaned back and belched, an attention-drawing sound that shook the table and threatened to draw a giggle from Karliah. "I don't suppose you're bringing me along to confirm its authenticity."

Appa's expression remained steady, professional, as he locked gazes with Barky and said, "Who else would cook for me? You know I can't last three days onboard with shit food."

Barky's mouth quirked upward. A laugh like Feasting Moon thunderstorms filled the booth as Appa exchanged his controlled demeanor for a lightheartedness rarely seen by even his closest friends. Karliah was happy to count herself among them.

"I want details," Barky said, leaning over the table once again. His voice was barely audible above the commotion of the inn. "But not here. For now, just tell me how soon you want to leave, and I'll arrange the crew and a meeting place."

Appa nodded, rose from the booth. "That'll depend on Zorah's success in locating our heading."

"Zorah." Barky turned Amma's name over in his mouth slowly, as if assessing the freshness of meat. "I don't suppose this has anything to do with her awskada associations."

Appa's lips pulled back, baring his teeth in a smile that didn't quite reach his eyes. "Only everything."

KONAR

The sun hovered just above the horizon, cutting a golden-pink path across the otherwise darkening waters. For the first time that day, Konar removed his hat—a smaller, simpler version of Appa's—and mopped his face with the excess fabric of his sleeve, allowing the wind to dry off what remained. He'd already taken liberty of his boots, rolled his pants up to his knees, and dangled each leg over the sides of the yasaaka where it tapered near the nose. Warm currents pulled at his feet and, from time to time, tiny fish nibbled his toes. Nothing dangerous lingered this close to the shallows, so Konar enjoyed the feeling without speculating about what slick-bodied creatures glided beneath him.

Mostly.

"If you're not going to help paddle, you could at least stop slowing me down with those flippers you call feet. You add enough weight as it is."

Despite Amma's scolding, there was a lightness in her voice. Konar drew his feet up and turned his body in one fluid motion, settling cross-legged, facing her. She stood tall, a head wrap masking the nyrian white of her hair, the wind blowing her skirts and blouse against her lean and muscular frame, one long paddle in hand as she guided them around the coast. As flawless as the sea goddess herself, save for the occasional hand to her temples to massage away the hangover ailing her.

"I suppose I could use them to paddle," he said, hovering one of his feet just above the surface.

Amma rolled her eye, then slapped the top of his foot with the paddle as he made to lower it. Konar grabbed the handle, gave it a tug. Amma held firm.

"Don't be so stubborn, Amma. Let me paddle. I'm not a boy anymore."

The corner of her eye creased, but she relinquished the paddle. "You'll always be my boy."

They traded places with precision, the yasaaka trembling only slightly under their shifting weight. Konar pulled them through the water, nearly doubling Amma's pace, and though she studied him with a hardened frown as he worked, there was admiration in it.

"Slow down," she said, even as she propped her arms behind her, tipping her head back to enjoy the breeze. "There's no one here to impress."

Konar felt his cheeks lifting. "This isn't even my full speed."

"Aye." She dipped her fingers in the water and came back with a handful of glimmering kelp, a near gemstone shade of midnight blue. "Your Appa wishes you'd show half this much ambition on *The Umbra*."

A grimace replaced all trace of Konar's smile. Sailing was a chore. Too many people, too much commotion, the duties endless and the respite brief, but he never missed a chance to take the family yasaaka out along the coastline, be it for fishing or leisure. Appa frowned upon the little board-boat hybrid, insisting its only use was transportation, and anything beyond that was for simpler folk with no ambition. If Appa only knew how much ambition it actually took to set off alone with nothing but one's mind and the seahawks for company, to balance body and gear atop a flat surface, to embrace one's insignificance against the thrashing waves and endless horizon.

But Appa never would. Appa knew best, knew all, and there was no telling him otherwise.

"I, however, don't care where you direct your ambition," Amma said, the deep notes of her voice breaking the silence. "In fact, I don't care if you have it at all. The world could do with fewer ambitious people. What it needs is more folks dedicated to living quiet lives, ones that don't leave damage when they're gone."

Konar guided the yasaaka to the shore, where the glittering fires from huts shone like starflies in the jungle. "And what am I, Amma? A man of ambition, or the quiet life?"

Amma faced the approaching coastline. "You've always been a curious boy, Konar. Full of questions and silent speculation." She peered over her shoulder at him, gave him a wink. "Don't let your skepticism poison you against the world. There's always some good in it, in people. I promise."

"So you say." Konar winked back and paddled the rest of the way in silence.

Their destination was a cove up the eastern coast from the village of Tongura. Since it was the smallest and most remote population on the main island of Zelos, the journey was made shorter by paddling along the coastline instead of cutting through the jungle. Konar was glad to skip the trek. There were no spiders with paralytic venom or rash-inducing flowers to dodge on the ocean—at least, not above water.

The cove itself had no name, for the awskada never named their settlements. Something to do with their belief that nothing was truly owned. The ghost of a village was observable from the bay and contained only a dozen or so huts that looked as if they'd collapse under the weakest of winds, save for one that towered high above the rest. A long, sun-bleached path of rickety bugana planking wound around the side of the island and up a cliff choked with overhanging greenery. Nevethium lanterns lit the way, a luxury Konar had only witnessed on brief and infrequent trips to Cadar for trade exchanges on neutral territory. Atop the cliff towered the mother of all the huts, which belonged to the mother of all awskada. At least the oldest living one.

Despite the warmth still lingering in the air, Konar shivered.

An arzok's shadow drifted over him, its leathery wings momentarily blocking the moonlight. Konar directed his attention to the skies, but the creature vanished into the canopy of trees before he determined its identity—not that he was exceptionally skilled at differentiating them. Most arzoks bore strong similarities to one another in terms of appearance. And though spotting one of the nocturnal creatures fishing at night was hardly an abnormality, few were bonded to anyone on their native islands.

Still, he had a strong feeling it was the one loyal to Amma. Her arzok never strayed far from her side, especially when she ventured outside Tongura under the anonymity of darkness. Their bond was more than reciprocal, more than an agreement to aid each other and help protect their mutual island home, more than the large cuts of meat Amma left out for him or the scouting services he provided on the open sea. It was the way she tended to his pups when their amma had died shortly after birth; the way he'd attacked a man who drunkenly lurched at Amma from an alley outside The Siren's Song when Appa was away on a voyage. And the way he let Konar stroke the silken fur underneath his neck when most arzoks wouldn't let anyone outside their bonded touch them at all.

Konar paddled faster, his mind swirling with ideas of what his eventual relationship with his arzok might be like. It wouldn't be long before he'd make the treacherous climb to the caves atop Zelos's largest mountain, a feat attempted by many ambitious youths eager to earn a coveted friendship with one of the creatures of the night. But even if he made it in one piece, there was no guarantee the arzoks would welcome an outsider with kindness, much less entrust one of their young to leave the family unit earlier than normal. Amma assured Konar he would pass whatever instinctual test they used to judge him, but the closer he drew to his thirteenth arrival day, the more anxious he grew.

"Boy!"

Konar stiffened at Amma's shout, gripping his toes into the yasaaka just before it ran aground. Amma clung to the sides as she leveled a glare at him.

"Get your wits about you, or I'll leave you here." Amma brushed off her clothes, even though the incident had done nothing to dirty them, and set off across the beach toward the nevethium-lit path, leaving soft impressions in the sand behind her.

Konar considered her words. He was in no hurry to meet his first real awskada, no matter how close Amma was with this particular one. They were harbingers for the goddesses, messengers from Quorath itself, and such power and wisdom came at a cost to both them and the people they benefitted. Konar didn't know what cost, exactly, but he'd read enough to know that—save for the direst of times—he'd do well to maintain a respectful distance from the supernatural.

Evidently, it was one of those dire times, at least according to Appa. And Konar wasn't about to let Amma face it alone.

Amma was a quarter way up the steps by the time Konar reached the dock beneath the awskada's hut (the dock he should've paddled them to, though Amma was gracious enough not to bring up his absentminded state that ran them aground in the sand a few yards to the west). The steps were slick with moss and seahawk droppings but surprisingly sturdy, and Konar only found one spot as he climbed that might soon fall victim to rot. Bugana wasn't lyvium, but it was incredibly water resistant and easily the sturdiest building material available on the islands.

To call the awskada's dwelling a hut was an understatement, for it was impressive even by Brune family standards with its four levels, each complete with a wraparound deck and littered with hanging plants, herbs, and caged birds. The latter appeared to be mostly local and known to him, common birds like seahawks and ravagers with the occasional siren thrown in. But Konar also spotted a much coveted tuross. The flying lizards weren't exactly exotic, but they were rare enough in Zelos that only the rich or powerful possessed them for long-distance communication. Konar assumed this awskada met both requirements.

"Oi, Konar, don't make me regret bringing you along."

Amma waited at the threshold of a simple yet well-made door, her figure shrouded by the gooey tentacles of a death-drop. The translucent beads the carnivorous plants produced appeared—to the eyes of common bugs and birds—to be water or dewdrops when, in reality, the substance was far stickier and poisonous. Prey became trapped in the gel, and then the plant would slowly recoil its tentacles, drawing the helpless creatures into its pitcher-shaped tomb where they were slowly digested for days. Deathdrops couldn't do much to larger beings besides giving a little sting equivalent to a mild bug bite, but their presence outside the hut's primary entrance said enough.

"Knock," Amma commanded, and Konar complied with three sharp raps.

Something inside growled. Konar stepped back, careful to avoid the grasping tentacles of the deathdrop, as the handle cocked to the right and the door swung inward, revealing a room so thick with green-tinted smoke that he couldn't see anything beyond the person greeting them.

Greeting was a bit of an overstatement. The woman who stood in the doorway was gaunt and spindly with long, beckoning fingers. Markings covered her body in the ink of a mizol, a brilliant white covering her upper chest, neck, and the lower half of her face in swirls every bit as unruly as waves in a storm. Thick, jagged lines of black were stitched over her full lips, ink as well, but the effect no less real. The skin of her exposed shoulders was nearly as black as the lines on her lips, and around her neck rested a lyvium chain, intertwined with sinuous vines and adorned with runes foreign to Konar. From it dangled tiny charms: three crescent moons, a vial of shimmering stardust, and an arzok with deep, iridescent gem eyes, capturing the essence of a moonlit ocean. At the heart of the necklace lay a smoothly cut piece of nevethium, its edges rounded into the shape of an eye. It wasn't the vibrant green he was used to seeing, however. Its glow was brighter, warmer, a yellow-green instead of the usual deep, forest green. It had a distinct hum not so unlike a distant swarm of insects. Konar wanted to rip it from her neck, hold it close to his beating heart.

Another part of him wanted to cast it into the sea.

"My wholeness to you, Grandamma," Amma said, breaking the silence.

"And your wholeness in mine, my child," the woman replied.

Her voice slithered out of her mouth and coiled around Konar in warm, pulsing waves. A voice soft as the silken sands of Zelos beaches, as calming as an amma whispering to a newborn babe, yet as strong as the western winds and alluring as a fire on a stormy night. He searched for her eyes, wanting desperately to know the owner of such a voice.

They were not his to behold. A great length of fabric was wrapped around the awskada's face, from her eyes to the top of her head, masking any hint of her race or beauty. Her spider–leg fingers fanned around the crystal at the head of her necklace, long, tattooed digits wrapping around it one by one.

Amma's elbow jabbed into Konar's side. He attempted a dry swallow and wished he'd heeded Amma's wisdom of packing a pouch of water (among other supplies) instead of spending the final moments leading up to their departure reading.

"My essence for yours, Grandamma," he whispered, using the greeting Amma had taught him. "We swear our lives upon yours, that it may never end."

The woman offered a short *hmm*, then moved aside so they could enter. Amma cast a glance at Konar from the side of her eye, a look not entirely disapproving in nature, and ventured into the awskada's realm. Konar found himself wishing Karliah was there with him. She would've loved to visit, to whisper and point at all the awskada's otherworldly possessions, to say the things Konar would never dare speak aloud. But Amma thought her too young, too reckless.

He wondered if he didn't fit those criteria himself.

A heavy air smothered the awskada's hut. It smelled of fire and spices and unwashed clothes. There was nowhere to sit, save for a pile of blankets beside the firepit (occupied by a scrawny mutt with its tongue hanging out) and a cot so worn and saggy in the middle that it looked more like a chair than a bed. Tables of varying sizes and heights cluttered the room, and the largest, the one that appeared to be the awskada's primary work station, was hidden beneath jars and pots, herbs and meats, animal skins and furs, and an assortment of gems and skulls. Cobwebs adorned nearly every corner, and some freshly made webs containing large, red flecked spiders filled others. The awskada glided over to the fireplace and began stirring a large cast-iron pot that looked, at least from the outside, as though it'd never been cleaned. The dog raised a lazy eyelid at her, then returned to its dozing.

"I know why you're here, Zorah of Eskos."

Old magic, Konar thought, unsure of how else the awskada could know the purpose of their visit. He sensed it in the reverberating tenor of her voice, as though anything in the room would bend to her will without hesitation.

Amma drew a sharp breath in through her nose. "He's already approached you?"

Or that. Konar silently scolded his weak mind for jumping to conclusions as he inched closer to the table, searching for anything... exciting? Otherworldly? Unnatural?

The awskada emitted what was presumably a laugh, but it sounded more like the shriek of a dying ravager bird. "*He* wouldn't dare set foot in this sanctuary. He knows his kind is unwelcome." She plucked a jar from the table, popped the cork, lifted it to her nose and, after taking a whiff that resulted in a soured expression, dumped it in the pot. "I received a tuross."

"And you refused him?" Amma asked.

"I don't work with, or for, tyrants, no matter how much they promise. Kept the tuross as a gift for the inconvenience, though." The awskada cackled again and grabbed a dust-covered bowl from one of the overhanging shelves, working quickly to ladle in a thick, gray substance of questionable texture.

"If you knew why I was coming..." Amma accepted the bowl thrust at her with a forced smile but kept it a safe distance from her face. "Then why allow me here at all? I may not be the emperor, but I ultimately come on his behalf."

"Must I have a reason to host one of my wayward children?"

Amma looked away before Konar could make out her expression.

He fought back a grimace as the awskada passed a bowl into his hands. A greasy, dusty film covered its exterior, and its contents smelled of fish gone bad mixed with rotten pyanne. The awskada neglected to serve herself any and drew her cot closer to the fire. She sat facing them, and though she still wore the head wrap masking her eyes, Konar felt her gaze boring into him with a heat to rival the flames. He lifted the bowl to his lips and sipped. The flavor actually wasn't all that awful, not unlike many fish stews he'd tasted at The Siren's Song, but the texture was enough to trigger a gag. He swallowed it, then took another sip for good measure. A crack of a smile sprung to life on the awskada's tattooed lips.

"We won't keep you," Amma said, stepping over the debris and bones on the floor to place her bowl on the table. "Your work is important, and I don't wish to be the target of your ill will regarding this job. I tried to reason Kor out of this foolish pursuit, but there's no stopping men when greed or lust sets their blood to boil. I don't have to be a part of it, though."

"If you don't do it, someone else will." The awskada hovered her hand above the flames, slowly turning it this way and that, as though she roasted a boar. If Konar hadn't known better, he would've sworn the fire followed her movement. "The scrolls no longer wish to remain hidden. They itch to fulfill their purposes." She grabbed Amma's bowl and placed it on the floor beside the dog. "Someone else will find them soon enough," she repeated, stroking the mutt as it lapped up the stew. "Better you. Better one of our kind."

By *our kind*, Konar didn't suppose she meant a fellow nyrian. He knew little of Amma's life before she met Appa, but he'd enough common sense about him to arrange the tidbits into a believable history. Amma was destined to be an awskada, had even spent many years of her life training to partake in whatever ritual ordained them. But Appa changed all that.

Amma and the awskada faced each other, the air thick between them, the room alive with the hum of the gem and the crackling of fire. Konar had a sudden urge to reach out and grasp his amma's hand, to pull her out of whatever spell the awskada had put her under, but then a single tear rolled down Amma's cheek.

"I cannot," she whispered. "I've abandoned our ways."

"They've not abandoned you." The awskada spoke with an air of reverence as she retrieved herbs from her table and set to work with a mortar and pestle in her lap. "My vows prevent me from disclosing the location of a relic that could harm countless lives, no matter how noble your intent. Neither can any of your ammas or setatas aid you in finding it. But you never took the vows." She glanced up, or rather her chin raised to imply such an action, and then it was Amma grabbing Konar's hand with a clammy grip.

"The spells will not bow to my whims," Amma persisted. She took a hesitant step toward the door as the awskada grabbed tiny bones from a shelf and ground them into the mixture.

"That is a risk you'll have to take."

A cool, slippery speech fell from the awskada lips, and the fire shivered in response, its flames shrinking. Another bottle went into the mortar, a dark, syrupy liquid. Konar was about to let himself out of the hut while they finished their discussion when the awskada shot a bony arm toward a perch suspended above the table, snatching an unsuspecting siren from its roost. She broke its neck the way one might crack eggs, then used one of her razor-sharp fingernails to spill blood from its tiny throat.

Konar's stomach dropped.

"Already, they hunt us," the awskada said as she poured the mixture into a crudely sculpted bottle. She corked it with care and passed it to Konar, then grasped Amma's hands in her own. "The emperor has enslaved every awskada who's refused him and tortures them to death, for he doesn't understand the goddesses won't allow us to break the very rules they set into existence. He'll continue to eradicate us one by one until the scroll is found." The awskada drew Amma close enough that their foreheads touched, then used her thumb to brush the tears still wet on Amma's cheek. "When you find it, Zorah, you must not give it to him, nor should he receive confirmation of its existence. Hide it from your partner if you must. Sacrifice everything to keep it in hands you deem safe. Better yet, destroy it. Quinaria is not ready to reap what those scrolls will sow."

Amma was a child in the awskada's arms, limp and slouching, eye wide and uncertain. "I'll bring it to you," she stammered. "You can take it into the caves."

The awskada's full lips parted, allowing a breathy sigh to escape. "I would much like to lay hands upon it. To taste the power of Quorath itself. But the scrolls aren't possessions to be admired or artifacts to study. They will fight to be used until they've fulfilled their purpose."

"And that is?" Konar blurted, drawing the attention of both women to him. He shrunk under the power radiating from them, wanted to cower for inserting himself into a conversation he probably shouldn't have born witness to. But Amma and the awskada both smiled at him. Amma's smile was warm and filled with pride.

The awskada's was predatory.

"That is for another time," they replied in unison, then chuckled to each other, grasping hands once again.

"Tell me what to do," Amma implored. "I'm ready for anything."

"I will aid you as much as I can," the awskada replied, turning toward the flames. A *pop* sounded from the fire, and a shower of embers fell over her like rain. She didn't flinch. Hardly seemed to notice the sparks at all. "But most will be left to your learnings. To the instinct still present within you. But, my child..." A thread of emotion choked her voice, and Konar caught a glimpse of the woman beneath the guise, of the life lost to servitude of another, even if it was of her own volition. "It will ask of you the one thing you're not ready to give."

A screech pierced the night, then another, cut short by whatever predator had ended its prey's life in the nearby jungle. Konar tried to make nothing of it. Coincidence was all.

Amma set her jaw. "It's the least I can do in repayment for the gifts I've squandered."

"So it is." The awskada made no attempt to mask her sorrow. "And yet, it will never be enough."

KARLIAH

I t wasn't the shouting that woke Karliah from her fitful sleep; though that was what caused her eyes to snap open, searching the glow of firelight streaming underneath the door of the room she shared with her bretata for signs of movement without. Nor was it the sound of a bottle shattering; though that did make her sit upright in her cot, fingers gripping the thin sheet she wore more for the idea of a covering than an actual need for warmth.

No, what yanked her out of her recurring nightmare of the angry, monstrous bear with teal smoke pouring from its nostrils was the *thunk* of her door shutting.

Amma and Appa preferred the doors within the hut open. They liked to know what was going on with her and Konar, to hear any would-be intruders that slipped past the attentive ears of their arzoks. But when they were about to have what they called an 'adult discussion,' one of them would close the door, sparing their children from the feuding. Or so they thought.

Karliah balled up her sheet, readying herself to hurl it across the room at Konar. She stopped mid-throw. Her bretata stood beside the door in his breeches and a loose nightshirt, ear pressed to the crack, a finger to his lips to warn her.

As if she needed a warning.

She lowered one foot silently to the ground, then the other, following a well-known path that avoided all the creaking floorboards. It hardly mattered. Amma and Appa had already escalated to a point in the argument where she could've stomped over in her boots without being noticed. She pressed her ear to the door opposite Konar and listened.

"You were the one who suggested I go to her," Amma slurred. She was at least a bottle in, maybe more.

"And make her do her demons' work, not you." Appa's voice was lower, more controlled. But it also had more venom behind it.

"Do you want the scroll or not? I'm the *only* one who can find it."

"Whatever makes you feel special, Zorah."

"You fucking..."

Amma's insult faded, likely drowned out by a drink. For a moment, the only sounds were the chirps of insects and the songs of sirens. A miracle, really. There were more nights than Karliah could count where they'd gone beyond the civility of talk and into the realm of violence. This time, they both sounded more sad than angry, as if they dreaded the inevitable and wanted the other to bear the brunt of the burden.

A bottle clattered to the floor, had likely slipped through Amma's fingers. Then, a sob. Footsteps clunking across the room. A shadow under the door. Konar and Karliah peeled away in unison, holding a collective breath until Appa's shadow vanished. He whispered something. Amma sobbed louder. The rest of their conversation remained a mystery, and soon their voices and footsteps faded.

Konar wrapped his arm around Karliah's shoulders.

"What did you hear before I woke?" she asked, voice still thick with sleep.

He shrugged. "More of what I already told you from our visit with the awskada. Amma told him what she said, what she thinks she needs to do. Appa didn't like it. Spoke ill of Amma's past, of awskadas in general."

Karliah's lower lip jutted out. "Why didn't you wake me sooner?"

"Didn't want the lack of sleep to make you even crankier than normal." Konar flopped back onto his cot, grinning, and made a great ordeal of pretending to fall asleep, complete with fake snores.

Karliah projected as much superficial hate as she could muster into a glare, but a smirk slipped through all the same.

The next morning, sun pierced through the windows in long, golden spears, and Appa and Amma puttered around the hut as if nothing was out of the ordinary, as if they weren't getting ready to set sail on the voyage of a lifetime or host a sacred ritual in their home. There was fried fish for breakfast, accompanied by Amma's melancholy humming. A list of tasks from Appa, along with a kiss on the cheek for Karliah as he headed out the door, an empty sack in one hand and a whistled tune on his lips. Karliah caught a cautious look from Konar as he shook his head at the unsettling normalcy of it all.

"I almost wish they were still fighting," he whispered to her between bites of fish when Amma stepped outside to share some scraps with her arzok. "Anything would be better than these forced pleasantries."

Karliah wasn't sure she agreed. Anything was preferential to the instability caused by their parents' fighting, even if it was all a lie. If her world was going to crumble around her, she didn't want to live in that reality any sooner than was necessary.

Konar frowned, swallowed the rest of his fish in three heaping bites, and left the hut with his boots slung over his shoulder. His leather-bound book lay beside his abandoned spot at the table. Karliah couldn't remember the last time he went anywhere without a book, and the knot in her stomach drew tighter.

"Are you sure I can't help with anything, Amma?" she asked as she was shooed out the door soon after.

Amma's smile didn't reach her eyes. She wrung and rubbed her hands the way she did when applying oil to smooth her skin. Only this time, there was no oil. "You can help me by helping yourself. Here's some aspar. Get a meal from Barky, visit old Chryia, find some new shells for your collection."

In other words, stay away from everyone and everything of importance. It was a wonder Amma even suggested Barky. Wouldn't he be busy, too?

"I could help Konar gather items for tonight. If you—"

"Go play, Karliah."

The door closed with an affirming *thud*.

Karliah went about her day as best she could, as if it was any other day. There were no Az Zarian highborns pulling into port, but she decided that was a good thing, given how last time turned out. Not that she was done with that little hobby. Just not now, not right before the job to end all jobs, as Appa called it. Especially when the job came from the most highborn of all Az Zarian highborns: the great emperor himself.

It was always exciting to have her parents called upon by the most powerful person in Quinaria. The closest thing they had on Zelos was the rujpati; though, they were practically Az Zarian highborns themselves, appointed by the emperor and responsible for upholding law and order since long before Appa's appa was born. Most of her people hated the rujpati, and they hated the emperor more. How Zelos came to be under Az Zar's control was the subject of much rage when the adults got to drinking. But she knew despite their nations' toxic history, it made Appa proud to be chosen by the emperor time and time again for work, even if it was the sort of work others might have moral qualms about.

Appa wasn't exactly known for work of the reputable sort, anyway.

Barky wasn't at The Siren's Song, and that was just as well. He would've treated Karliah the same as her parents and bretata did. A little pat on the head, a little treat to stay out of the way, a little forced jealousy to remind her how lucky she was to still be so small, so young, so innocent.

Right. Because a child of pirates lived a life of blissful ignorance. She wouldn't have cared so much if they'd regularly excluded her from their less than savory endeavors, but when they not only allowed but even expected her to help with family business, it made any rejection feel more like a slight.

Maybe Chryia would show her some well-deserved respect. It wasn't as if the old woman had much to brag about, anyway.

Karliah strutted into village center, wincing at the sunlight reflecting off the lyvium-plated features of the fountain. She hurried over to the scant shade offered by the worn fabric loosely drawn over Chryia's cart, careful to avoid the beams of light cast from the overhead sun through the holes.

"Didn't 'spect ya so soon, dearie," Chryia said as Karliah peered down at her loot.

"Soon?" Karliah asked, selecting a shell to examine. Chryia didn't solely make her living from shells. There were sunstones to help track the passage of time (a ruse), herbs that helped people make babies (or get rid of them), ancient cups as old as Quinaria (the ancient part a lie to excuse their poor quality), and woven hair ties (cut up pieces of nicer blankets she'd burned or sealed with wax on the ends). The shells weren't farce, though, and the one she held was nearly translucent and shaped like a waning moon.

"Your amma didn't tell you?"

The shell had an opening on one end, and when she put her finger inside, it was... velvety? "Tell me what?" she asked, forgetting how the conversation had even begun.

"That yer staying with me tonight, girl. And the next few nights after that, for however long it takes. Room and board in exchange for yer help with the cart while your family's away."

Karliah's fingers closed around the shell. She searched the old woman's wrinkled, sun-spotted face for any hints of teasing, but Chryia's cracked lips were pinched together in a no-nonsense sort of way, one white eyebrow raised over an eye that was milky with blindness.

"But I'm supposed to be back home by sundown," Karliah said, bending down to adjust the laces on her boots—and slip the shell into her billowing sleeve. *Never miss an opportunity,* she imagined Appa saying as he smiled over her shoulder.

"Probably to get yer things," Chryia said with a shrug. "They didn't want you over there tonight, that I know."

"Oh."

Karliah steadied her bubbling emotions with a calming breath. It didn't come easily to her yet, but she was learning when to let them loose and when to stifle them to gain an advantage. This was one of those times.

She took a few more breaths, and when the rage abated, she turned a smile on Chryia. "Tonight, then. I'll bring you some fried fish. Amma cooked up a whole batch this morning."

Chryia's mouth opened into a toothless grin. "Aye, she always cooks them so soft and flakey, your amma does. I look forward to your company, girl. Now, off with you."

Karliah blew a kiss as she skipped between carts and down the street. Only when she rounded the corner into the alleyway behind The Siren's Song did she let out a muffled scream.

How dare they leave her behind. Didn't they realize she was happiest with them, not to mention the safest? What could old Chryia do if one of Appa's angry debtors came seeking revenge for his strict contracts? Or what if a highborn she'd wronged managed to track her down?

And Konar. He knew. He had to know. And he didn't tell her. Sat right next to her over fried fish and whined about the overly pleasant morning instead of telling her *why*, truly why.

Karliah withdrew the shell from her sleeve and rubbed its smooth surface against her cheek, savoring the coolness it transferred to her skin. Another challenge, that's all this was.

And she was ready for it.

No outsiders joined the Brune hut that night. Karliah shouldn't have been surprised; Appa didn't exactly want anyone to know of Amma's would-have-been-awskada past, probably because it threatened to diminish his own status. Or out of fear that people might try to use her lingering gifts to their own advantage.

Not that there was anything to use.

If Amma had any gifts, Karliah hadn't seen them. Sure, she knew the best way to treat any illness or wound, had a way with animals, could name any plant and list their properties and uses, could tell stories so vividly that Karliah found herself questioning if they were not actually unfolding before her eyes.

But none of that was magic. Konar was well on his way to learning half of those things in his books. Still, an awskada at work was nothing to miss, even for the skeptical people of Tongura. A chance at prolonged life, newfound wealth, or a glimpse into one's future was well worth the risk. And Appa had gone to great lengths to hide the ritual, had insisted Amma hold it indoors within the protection of their hut's walls when it was normally conducted under the guidance of the moons. That much Karliah had picked up from their heated discussion over the morning meal.

It was all irrelevant, anyway. All that mattered was that she was finally about to learn whether Amma had real magic.

Karliah adjusted her position in the net she'd secured to the bottom of the hut. She'd gone home immediately after her discussion with Chryia and retrieved an abandoned fishing net she'd tucked away moons ago for reasons not then known to her—she was always hiding away rejected and pilfered things—then went to work securing it to the bottom of the hut. There was a spot beneath the family room that was mostly hidden by decorative grasses hanging from the porch and, given the fact the net was thin and her family would likely be home as the light began to fade and affect vision, she took the risk of positioning it there. A nice spot, just under the loose floorboards, where there were plenty of cracks. It wasn't the sturdiest nest, and she nearly fell twice as she reached out from between the steps to nail it in, body teetering and nothing but a rope around her waist to prevent the thirty-foot fall. She tried not to think about what would happen if she lost her balance, tried not to question the rope's integrity. And when it was all said and done, she wore a sheen of sweat and pride for her efforts.

"Konar shouldn't be here either," Appa was saying, not three feet above where Karliah hid. His heavy footsteps faded away, followed by the groan of their great sun-blood table sliding across the floor. "It's not too late to send him to Chryia's."

"If he's man enough to accompany us on the voyage, he's more than ready to bear witness to this," Amma replied, dragging what sounded like two of the chairs in the direction Appa had gone. There was no slur in her voice tonight. In fact, Karliah couldn't recall the last time she'd sensed such a calmness about her.

Appa grunted, and the sound of his footsteps vanished. Either he'd taken off his boots and slung his feet onto the table to observe, or he'd left the room entirely. Not long after, softer, more intentional footsteps walked into the room, and Karliah caught a glimpse of her bretata through one of the cracks.

"Here are the things you requested, Amma," he said.

There was no speech amidst the jostling of whatever objects were handed off to Amma, and Karliah arched her neck as far outside the net as possible in hopes of stealing a peek. It was for naught. With a huff, she settled back comfortably into the net and shut her eyes to better listen.

She stifled an excited gasp as something shrieked. It sounded awfully like a gwanei. Their shrill screams and occasional coughing honks were unmistakable.

"It's not even full grown," Konar said with a heaviness beyond his years. "I searched for an elderly one, but there weren't any around. The nest was abandoned, probably because it was so far up that cliff, and there were so many, too many... I didn't think they'd miss one..."

The shrieking increased in intensity, drowning Konar's voice, but Karliah figured he'd run out of things to say, anyway.

"It's alright," Amma shouted over the noise. "You did your best." Karliah tracked the shadow of her body through the cracks as she crossed the room. "And you?" Amma said, her voice less forgiving. "Where are your contributions?"

Something thudded, but not on the ground. Karliah risked leaning out of the net to peer through a different crack and watched as Appa rifled through a sack on the table. He withdrew something slimy and dark that was roughly the size of his fist. He plopped it onto the table, wiped his hand on his pants in disgust, then reached into the sack again. This time, his hand emerged with a bound parchment sealed with wax.

"What's that?" Amma shouted. She turned, revealing the writhing gwanei in her hands, and thrust it back to Konar. "Silence it," she said, the calmness in her voice threatening to dissipate.

"A map," Appa replied with a shrug. He reached inside his coat pocket where he kept his pipe, but Amma must've given him a look, for his hand reemerged empty. "New isles charted to the south of Orillon. At least that's what Barky's supplier believes. You don't want to know how much aspar it cost us, either."

"It won't matter if this goes to plan." Amma slipped the parchment into the opening of her blouse. The shrieking had stopped, and Karliah wondered if the creature was merely silenced or if her bretata had permanently addressed the problem.

Appa folded his arms and chewed his bottom lip in place of the pipe. "And where are your contributions?"

"That's not your concern." Amma walked away from Karliah's view, and the light within the hut began to dim. "Neither of you are to speak once I begin the ritual." Her voice was muffled, as if she'd gone into another room.

Ages passed by with nothing but the sounds of the night to serenade Karliah while she waited. Her grasp on time was fluid, each breath an eternity, the moons above unmoving, unwilling to acknowledge she'd waited more than long enough for something, anything, to happen, only for it to come racing at her in a rush of emotions and heat when the floorboards above her groaned under the weight of one of her family members. A deep singing broke the hut's silence, a tune so favored by Amma that she'd used it to introduce a much younger Karliah to the ancient awskada tongue:

Breathe through me, and I
through you

No mortal can loosen bonds
that are true

Rest now your spirit, take
flight with mine

What once was always is,
forever intertwined

An odd scent seeped through the boards and wafted over Karliah's face. She couldn't quite place it. It had the essence of smoke, but it smelled sweeter, almost sickly sweet, as though the fragrance clung to the fine hairs inside her nose. It left a bitter taste on the back of her tongue, and she cleared her throat to rid it from her mouth, hoping the manner in which she did so was discreet enough.

It wasn't. Someone came to stand right above her. Heart thudding, she shirked away from the larger hole in the floorboard as a violet eye slowly widened in recognition. Her lower lip bulged, hands folded into a plea as Konar looked from her to the room and back to her again. His face remained unchanged as he drifted toward the hole and covered it with his foot.

Karliah cursed him under her breath. He was only protecting her, but in doing so he sealed off her best vantage point. She shifted in the net, gaze roving over each floorboard and every crack for a weakness, but the darkened room left her few options.

A change in Amma's song halted Karliah's meaningless search, and she lay back to listen, closing her eyes to better focus on the lyrics. The tune remained the same, but new verses flowed from Amma's lips, ones she'd never murmured over Karliah until now:

All you ask I give, for a chance
to behold

Those stolen gifts whose
resurgence is foretold

The heart of a lover, some-
thing new to discover

The touch of a mother, and
the soul of another

Take now my offerings, for-
give me at last

All ammas forever; present,
future, and past

Forsake not your kin, I am
yours to command

Fill me with your essence;
prepare me to stand

A light flashed inside as Amma finished her eerie tune. Someone cried out; Konar, given the surprise and register of the voice. The hole he'd been covering suddenly opened, and Karliah pressed her eye to the floorboard, no longer caring if she got caught.

Amma dipped a cup into a steaming, smoking cast-iron pot Karliah wasn't aware they owned, and as she removed the drinking vessel, a thick, oozy liquid trailed down the sides. Karliah held her breath as Amma raised it to her lips and drank.

The cup clattered to the floor. Amma grabbed the edges of the pot to steady herself and let out a long, anguished cry, her lips pulled back to reveal her flawless teeth. Karliah didn't realize she was screaming, too, until her throat ached and her lungs begged for air. She clamped a hand over her mouth, nearly losing her balance in the process. She locked a finger into the hole to steady herself, then slowly eased her body back upright.

Amma writhed on the floor, limbs flailing, her jaw clenched, her eye void of a pupil, its shade a startling white pure as a Feasting Moon. Appa and Konar kneeled beside her, each doing their best to soothe her by restricting her limbs and stroking the waves of her hair.

"Make it stop!" Konar shouted at Appa, his chin dimpling.

Appa replied with a stern gaze that seemed to say, *this was of her making, not mine.*

Karliah was ready to abandon her position, ready to do whatever it took to help Amma, even if it meant suffering through days with old Chryia, when Amma sucked in a breath that sounded half a scream. She heaved herself up on trembling arms, brushing off the help offered by Appa and Konar.

She sat there, knees drawn to her chest, the moonlight basking her in its ghostly glow, for what felt like an eternity. Then her eye shot open.

"I have seen," she croaked, "and I cannot unsee." No one dared press further as Amma rose on weak legs and stumbled to the window, out of Karliah's line of sight. But the words she spoke chilled Karliah all the same. "Much ill will come of this. I fear where this path will inevitably lead, but the responsibility now lies with this family, and in this family, the scrolls must remain." Footsteps sounded overhead, coming to stop above Karliah's hiding place. Amma kneeled and lowered her face to the floor. An eye the same greenish blue as Skyfall Sea appeared in the hole. "Karliah. Come. You've borne witness, and there is no escaping your duty. I didn't wish this for you, but clearly the fates have plans greater than mine."

As Karliah swung out of the net and onto the stairs, ascending them with her head hung and her fists clenching, a deep knot formed in her stomach. Something had changed, and though she didn't yet understand its severity, a small voice whispered in her head, one that was not her own.

The scrolls, it commanded. *Find the scrolls.*

KONAR

Appa's arzok soared above *The Umbra*, her immense wings veined with an eerie, ethereal glow, allowing her to glide through the darkness with unsettling grace and silence. She landed on the bowsprit and studied Konar with sharp, obsidian eyes peering from a face adorned with rows of serrated fangs, her expression betraying her intelligence. Her lithe yet muscular body was shrouded in a tapestry of midnight hues, gleaming like satin in the moonlight, and her long, whip-like tail, adorned with thorny spines, flicked back and forth.

Konar raised a hand in greeting, using the other to keep the pages of his book spread open so as to not lose his place. Appa's arzok craned her neck around in the impossible way her kind did, dropping her head nearly to her chest, her unblinking gaze locked on Konar, peering deep into his soul. Konar rose from his reclined position against the foremast and approached the creature, keeping his own gaze down. Arzoks demanded respect, but that was their right as fellow inhabitants of Quinaria. Konar had long since abandoned the conventional notion that the ability to speak was the sole determiner in marking one's intelligence, and though the sentiment was harder and harder to find among his peers, most of the world had understood it at one time or another. The book in his hand was proof, as was Appa's arzok ally. An arzok could sense whether another being still held such beliefs and knew that Konar was an extension of

Korandon Brune. And despite all Konar's qualms with Appa, he couldn't deny the man respected all forms of life.

For that, he had Konar's respect.

The arzok lowered her head toward Konar's open palm, velvety ears flattened but fangs kept safely hidden away. Konar held his breath and pushed his hand closer. He'd only stroked the magnificent creature twice in all his life, and just one more stroke would secure the confidence he needed to finally make the climb to bond with his own. After they returned from the mission, of course.

Konar had yet to make contact when the arzok's eyes widened suddenly, her broad, pointed ears flicking this way and that, her lips pulled back to reveal those dreadful fangs. Then, flexing a wingspan as long as Konar was tall, she took to the night.

It didn't take long to find out why. Light spilled onto the deck as an onslaught of drunken laughter shattered the otherwise soothing lapping of waves and the creaking of *The Umbra*. Konar slipped the book back into his vest and tried his hardest to appear busy with... well, watching, he supposed. That was technically all he'd been assigned to do. Keep an eye out for the place on the map that didn't exist for a scroll that didn't exist, all because Amma's vision said so. And even though he could keep watch perfectly fine by glancing up after every few pages, Appa wouldn't think so, wouldn't believe the job was efficient. And the crew would only ridicule him. Pirates didn't waste time aboard reading, especially not the son of the feared and terrible Brineheart. Not when there were decks to be swabbed and curses to be splattered about like bird shit.

A hand clapped onto Konar's back, and it was so thick and floppy (not to mention wet) that he could've easily mistaken it for a fish—in the unlikely event the crew were throwing fish about for entertainment, which he wouldn't put them above.

The hand in question, however, belonged to none other than Barthonax Azaila, or Barky, as he'd self-ordained long before Konar drew his first breath. He liked to imply he'd been given the nickname because he obsessively peeled the bark off zidel trees and chewed it, as if he was the only one to do so. Half the adult population of Zelos chewed or smoked the ground up bark for its clarity benefits and general feel-good sensations, and almost all the sailors Appa worked with were downright addicted. Unlike many others, however, it didn't stop Barky from being a skilled navigator and cook.

Konar could give him that.

He forced a concentrated look onto his face, as though he'd been interrupted while giving the ocean his undivided attention, then glanced over his shoulder at Barky. The cook wasn't alone. Azra stood at attention beside him, red eyes shifting, studying the deck, the ocean, the skies, for whatever evil might besiege them. He was always ready—always hoping—for a fight. Konar supposed that's what one did when one spent half a nyrian lifespan swinging curved swords for pleasure in between bouts of pillaging and drunken brawls. The two hundred pounds of muscle he rarely bothered to contain in a shirt probably didn't help to quell his urges, either.

"Evenin', Brineson," Barky said as he tipped back a bottle of kolaash.

Konar fought to keep the irritation from making its way to his face. The diminutive version of his Appa's pirate name wasn't intended as a compliment, especially given Konar's lack of... well, everything one might associate a pirate with.

"Evening," he said through clenched teeth.

Barky hiked his bad leg up onto a supply barrel and rubbed the spot on his calf where wood met flesh. "Missing all the excitement down below. A lad like yourself on the cusp of manhood should be drinking and making allies instead of being isolated up here." He bent over his leg in an awkward stretch, belly grazing the barrel. "I'll cover for ya, if you'd like. No one need know."

It might've been a test to see if Konar would speak ill of Appa's commands. It might've been a challenge to face the scenario Konar feared most: large gatherings. And there was the small possibility Barky actually cared, actually wanted to make sure Konar enjoyed himself on *The Umbra* this voyage.

Unlikely.

"Thank you, but my watch is almost done," he replied. Then, realizing that answer didn't benefit him in the slightest, added, "And I promised Karliah to..."

Azra's eyebrows raised as he shot a knowing glance over to Barky.

"... to help her with her reading tonight," Konar finished before they slid another remark in.

He *did* need to help Karliah with her reading and writing. She was nowhere near as capable as he'd been at her age, and he wasn't about to let his younger setata remain ignorant. Getting her to participate, however, was another matter. Even he only had so much sway over her, the stubborn little thing that she was, and throughout the entire fortnight they'd spent at sea, she'd only allowed him to give her one lesson. One. As if she had nothing better to do than harass the crew with her incessant questions and sneak into Appa's cabin to rifle through his things when he was otherwise occupied.

"'Course ya did, good bretata that ya are," Barky said, his tone not entirely mocking.

Someone else snickered, though, and the aggression didn't belong to Azra, who was too busy stealing a swig of Barky's kolaash. Konar searched the shadows behind them, his eyes blinking until they separated the form of another being from the darkness. Realization rippled down his spine in the form of prickled flesh.

Of course. Of course, it was him.

Konar's stomach clenched. There was only one aboard those glowing, slit-pupiled eyes could belong to.

Gerosa.

Wherever Appa went, Barky followed, and Azra followed Barky, which left Gerosa to follow Azra. Every job, every voyage.

Every reason Konar wanted to get as far away from the pirate life as possible.

One of the moons broke from the cloud cover, spilling a murky gray light onto the deck and illuminating Gerosa's towering frame. The beridian wasn't bulked with muscle, but his seven-foot height combined with his poisonous claws and the instincts of all his predator brethren made him far more intimidating than Azra—at least as far as Konar was concerned.

"Going to swing more than your mouth this voyage?" Gerosa asked in heavily accented Nyrinian. The beridian spoke many languages outside of his native Hispen, but he didn't know, and refused to learn, Zarith. Konar couldn't blame him in that regard. Az Zar's ill-treatment of Zelos was little more than a scratch compared to their animosity toward Gerosa's race.

"I've been practicing." Konar hoped the uncertainty in his heart didn't bleed into his voice.

Gerosa hopped down from the railing with innate grace and stalked toward Konar, his tail flicking behind him, his lyvium forearm guards glinting, proudly showcasing the fact they'd never been so much as scuffed—and not from lack of fighting. "Care to have a go now?" He bared his fangs in a joyless smile.

"The Brineheart won't stand for any brawling on his ship, whether it be in good humor or no." Barky shouldered the beridian in jest, but his eyes carried a warning. He gave Konar's shoulder a squeeze. "Go on, lad. Keep your setata company. I'm up for next watch and could use some salt-stained air starting now."

Konar didn't correct him on his poor word choice, not with the warm twinkle in Barky's eyes and the opportunity to *not* spend another moment in Gerosa's presence, thank you very much. He kept his gaze down as he arced around the beridian and brushed past Azra, the latter providing him with another slap on the back in parting. As far as Konar knew, Azra was indifferent to him. Not as fond as Barky or as full of hatred as Gerosa. But given the right, or rather, wrong, circumstances, that indifference could prove deadly.

It wasn't that Konar *liked* to think his Appa's closest partners, the sailors and allies he called upon for any and all undertakings, would kill him for the right price. It was the plain and simple truth. Gerosa had never forgiven him for the slip of his tongue that fateful night three years ago, and he never would. No matter that the consequences that followed hadn't been intentional, that Konar had only been nine at the time and not properly educated in the way adults conducted themselves. At least the adults Appa kept close.

How was he supposed to know *not* to run to the village center and alert the rujpati when he caught Gerosa dragging a muffled but still thrashing woman behind stacks of grime covered barrels on the docks? That despite Appa's insistence upon bringing Konar along to oversee a transaction, the Brineheart would slip away to meet with a lady friend while Amma nurtured a sick Karliah back home? Even Barky had been passed out in a drunken stupor, leaving Konar alone to witness the atrocity and fend for himself. He'd stood there on that dock, cold for the first time since he could remember, while what felt like hours crawled by.

It was likely only minutes.

And then the woman must've broken free for a moment, for she screamed a blood-chilling cry that was cut off abruptly. Dark blood pooled on the already stained dock and snaked toward Konar's feet with foreboding intent. Then two glimmering eyes peered over the barrels. They narrowed, unblinking. But Konar was already running, tears as salty as the ocean streaking down his cheeks. Gerosa didn't follow, perhaps didn't want to take the risk of explaining what happened to his captain's son had he silenced him then. But ever since, Konar knew he was marked. Given the chance, the beridian would kill him in the most painful way imaginable.

He shook his head to chase the memory away.

Most people had it wrong. Pirates were folk of integrity who held strongly to their morals. It was just that they created their own code of what they deemed right and wrong.

And Konar had broken it.

"You're certain, Zorah?"

"How certain do you think one can be with these kinds of things? Bah."

"Certain enough to take this costly voyage, I hope. The crew grows impatient. Promises of great wealth mean nothing without—"

"Don't you think I'm aware? I'm the one they cast hateful glances over their shoulders at. The one whose name they curse when they get to drinking." A pause, then, "They'd never dare speak such heresy of the Brineheart."

Konar pulled his hat tighter down over his face, almost wishing he'd taken up Appa's offer to sleep below deck to prove himself as a member of the crew. But *The Umbra* wasn't that large, and it wouldn't take long for Gerosa to discover him down there. He'd wait until Konar was asleep, and then...

It wouldn't help to dwell on it. Even if he bunked down there for a day or two and survived the ordeal, the crew wouldn't just miraculously accept him. Probably not ever. The light from the lantern, Amma and Appa's raised whispers that may as well have been shouts, Karliah's quiet little puffs of snores. It was all worth a warm, safe place to sleep, even if it hurt his reputation.

Konar had almost nodded off to sleep again when the sound of crinkling parchment marred the silence.

"You must have the location wrong," Appa said gruffly. "Neither of the arzoks are finding uncharted land. People have sailed around searching for the old myrem settlements for centuries. If there was land around here once, it's long since submerged."

"Then we dive."

"Are you the first volunteer?"

"Put your crew to use." Amma lingered on each word, slathering each one with a fresh heap of condescendence.

"Fine. You tell them."

Konar was wide awake by this point, all hope of sleep slipping through his fingers like water, when the cabin door shuddered under the weight of repeated pounding. He withdrew his hat from his face and tumbled out of the netted bed in one mostly smooth transition. Amma and Appa looked up from the map they'd bent over.

The door thundered again. This time Karliah sat up, eyes puffy with sleep.

"Captain Brineheart!" a muffled voice called through the thick wood. "We're under—"

Appa was already rolling up the map and shoving it into Amma's hands. "Zorah, Karliah: there are knives and daggers in the chest beside my cot. Arm yourselves and lock the door as soon as we leave. Only open it for me or Konar." The sound of Appa's sword sliding from its scabbard made the danger suddenly imminent, in case they had reason to doubt. "Boy!"

Konar's head buzzed as he dragged his feet toward Appa. It was a chance to prove himself, but if his racing heart was any sign, he wasn't ready.

"Korandon, no," Amma exhaled, moving to block the door. "Let him stay, he—"

"It's alright, Amma." Konar planted a kiss on her cheek, just below her eyepatch. The last thing his parents needed at that moment was another argument.

The sound of splintering wood silenced them. With it came more shouts. Appa retrieved a sword hanging from a plaque above the doorframe and passed it to Konar. A lyvium blade, like his appa's. A coveted metal native to Az Zar, and rare even there. The blade was straight and sleek, the handle made from the tusks of some great northern beast Appa had likely snatched on a raid. His fingers curled around it, trying to claim it, to command it the way Appa and the rest of the crew did.

He already felt it betraying him.

But then Appa was there, grabbing his collar, drawing Konar to him, forcing him to look into his deep violet eyes. Eyes the color of a Zelosi sunset.

"Don't leave my side. Trust your instincts. If you're unsure, swing to kill. Better someone else than you." Appa's warning marched out in one long, controlled breath.

Konar swallowed, couldn't get his dry throat to eke out a response.

Appa crushed Karliah in a hug and gave Amma the first genuine kiss Konar had seen them exchange in moons. "I'll be back. We'll be back." He unlatched the door and caught Amma's gaze with such intensity that Konar had to look away. "I love you."

"I know," Amma whispered, a pained smile on her lips.

Then Appa was lifting the latch, flinging open the door.

Dragging them into darkness.

The black deck of *The Umbra* was slick with rain. Konar didn't recall any drops pelting the cabin, any wind rattling the windows, but perhaps he'd been too distracted by Appa and Amma's argument to notice. Not that it qualified as a storm yet. The weather was forgiving, the air tepid, the rain gentle, not the kind that blew sideways and stabbed into one's skin. Even the ship's rocking had a gentle cadence.

Konar wished it was the worst storm of the century. Perhaps if it had been, he wouldn't have had to witness what lay just outside Appa's cabin.

He pressed his eyelids tightly together before forcing himself to look again. A sailor was on his knees, head drooped low over his chest like he'd fallen asleep in an awkward position, the way some did after a night of drinking. Perfectly normal, save for the handle of a javelin protruding from a red bloom on his back. The tip had wedged itself to the deck, keeping the man upright, and the rain was making quick work of the blood pooling around him, washing it against the perimeter of the cabin and beyond. Another sailor lay crumpled a few feet beyond, his neck sliced so deep that Konar was certain the slightest movement would finish detaching his head. He didn't recognize the man, hadn't seen him aboard *The Umbra* before.

The evening meal roiled in his stomach. How had they been boarded? Wasn't there someone, several people maybe, on watch? Who knew how many intruders now prowled aboard, slitting the throats of sleeping—

Appa slapped Konar's cheek, temporarily obscuring all thought.

"We've been boarded," Konar stammered, swallowing back bile.

"Obviously," Appa growled. "Whatever drunken halfwits Barky left on watch tonight are getting executed if they survive this. I told him to keep the crew off the booze, that this mission was too high risk." Appa's free hand balled into a fist. He drew a steadying breath through his nostrils, let it loose, then gave Konar's shoulder a squeeze. "Stay alert."

Konar numbly followed, still hindered by the buzzing in his ears, already wishing he'd not been concerned with proving his manhood and had stayed with Amma. Sounds of metal clanging and clashing drowned the night air, rivaled only by the cries of wounded and dying sailors. His head swiveled this way and that, gaze peering into the deepest shadows, begging the invaders to attack someone else, please. As he ran, his sword slipped from his grasp and slid a few feet across the deck. He looked down to find his hands shaking. His breath caught in his throat.

I'm not ready, Appa.

But Appa was sprinting ahead, kneeling to examine another body. Konar snatched the sword up, gripping it so tightly the skin on his knuckles stretched.

Move, he told himself. *This is not your time.*

And it wasn't. Somewhere deep down, he knew, and it gave him enough strength—nothing he'd so carelessly claim as courage—to hurry after Appa, despite every bit of his body begging him to turn around and seek refuge with Amma and Karliah.

He stopped to catch his breath a few feet away from the trapdoor leading to the lower deck, even though the distance hadn't been great, certainly not great enough to elicit any heavy breathing. Sailors stumbled up the ladder and out into the night, some clothed, some not; some armed, some not. Appa stood directly above the door, shouting at his crew to get a move on, to find and kill the invaders, to...

Konar stopped listening. A man emerged from the shadows, swinging through the air on a rope, and landed on the deck a few feet from Konar. He drew his blade, raised it above his head. His cold, lusterless eyes narrowed. Konar gripped his sword with both hands, holding it in front of him the way he'd been taught, his bare toes curling into the deck, but the man was almost on him, and he wasn't going to survive this, didn't stand a—

The man's mouth and eyes widened simultaneously as a blade sprang forth from his stomach. He grabbed at it, slicing up his hands until a dagger drew across his throat. The man—the body—went slack, and his killer yanked the blade free.

Barky.

The cook rushed to Konar and pulled him into a rough embrace.

"You alright then, lad?"

Konar couldn't will his arms to return the hug. He pulled free of Barky and studied the crimson stain running off his blade.

"Next time, don't think. Strike. You hear me?" When Konar yet again didn't reply, Barky gave him a little shake. "Boy!"

"Strike. Kill." The words sounded distant as Konar spoke them. He raised the sword, took a practice swing.

"Good." Barky slapped his back, this time not in jest, and caught Appa's arm as he tried to hurry past. "Competition," he said, using his chin to gesture to the body. "They must've slithered in on smaller boats to cause a distraction while the main ship drew within range. Our lower deck is compromised. Pierced with the largest arrow I've ever seen. The spearhead is—" Barky used his hands to show a length nearly as long as his arm span.

Appa nodded, not sparing so much as a moment to look Barky in the eyes. "The emperor isn't foolish enough to rely on us alone."

Lightning crackled overhead, briefly illuminating *The Umbra* in a burst of light, and the ship next to it. Konar shirked away as he took in the new ship's hulking form. It was at least twice the size of *The Umbra*, its masts carved to resemble tentacles, its burnt orange sails showcasing an eight-legged sea monster, and positioned on its starboard deck, facing them, were several of the largest crossbows Konar had ever seen. They weren't actually crossbows, but he didn't know what else to compare them to, had never even heard of such a thing.

As if it had been waiting for them to see, to know what was about to kill them, one launched with a resounding *twang* and a clattering of metal, sending another projectile into the side of *The Umbra*. The crew still trapped below screamed. Konar tried not to imagine it impaling any of the unfortunate sailors assigned to containing the leaks.

Several nearby *thuds* jerked Konar's attention back to his vulnerable body, back to the newly landed enemy pirates assaulting the deck like fleas on a dog. Appa crossed blades with one, spinning about the man with ease before using a backhanded attack to drive his blade into his opponent's stomach. Two more landed on either side of Appa. A dagger flew from Appa's hand so swiftly that Konar hadn't realized he'd thrown it until it embedded itself in the woman's eye. The other held his own with Appa, but only for a few seconds. Appa severed his head from his shoulders before pushing the crumpling body the rest of the way overboard with his boot.

But Appa didn't see the next one, the wraith of a woman creeping behind him with two bastard swords. Konar relied on impulse as he raced toward her from his hiding place in the shadows and drove his sword into her lower back with trembling hands. Her cry rang above the other shouts, above the now pelting rain. It halted him in his tracks. He backed away, his sword still lodged in her back. Another of the giant arrows struck the ship with enough force to send her sprawling forward. Appa, taking mere seconds to finish off his next kill, looked from Konar to the dying woman.

And the look he gave Konar made his heart swell.

"Retrieve your sword," he shouted over the commotion.

It took Konar a moment to wrench it free. He hardly minded the way it clung to the bone, didn't allow himself to notice how the blood seeped out like he'd just pulled the cork on a barrel of ale. He'd do it again and again and again if it meant Appa looked at him that way.

Barky appeared beside him, his apron splattered in blood. "Brineheart," he called out, hacking another enemy pirate with his cleaver until the man's face was shredded beyond recognition. "Azra says we can't sustain any more hits."

"Then we go over." Appa grabbed a plank, his arm rippling with muscle where the sleeve had torn off. Barky moved to help him, but Gerosa was already there, guiding it across.

For once, Konar was glad for the beridian's presence.

"Konar," Appa shouted as he dueled with a pirate crossing the plank from the opposite side. "Go look after your amma and Karliah. Protect them." With that, he vanished into the darkness that was the other ship.

Konar didn't need to be asked twice. He rushed past Barky, his heart sinking as he dodged Appa's crew, most of them caught in fights where they were outnumbered two to one. Even if Appa disabled the weapons, they still might not survive the—

Konar's vision faded as something cold and heavy smacked into the back of his head. He doubled over, ears ringing, slipping into darkness, cold darkness.

Then the pain stopped.

KARLIAH

Karliah hadn't moved since Appa and Konar abandoned her and Amma to the tomb that was the captain's quarters. She'd watched unblinking as Amma slid the door bar into place with a *thud* and rushed over to Appa's chest to retrieve weapons. Next thing she knew, Amma was thrusting a knife into her hands, and Karliah was examining it like it was one of Chryia's shells, marveling at its weight, at the way the blade was altogether too sharp, too dangerous for her tiny fingers, yet not sharp enough. Not sharp enough to do what it needed to do, should it come to that, to the thing little girls weren't supposed to know about—much less act upon.

Every time her pointed ears picked up another shout, Karliah shivered. Every time the ship trembled in a way that couldn't possibly have been caused by the waves, Karliah's body tensed. Every time Amma completed another circle around the room, her own daggers on display, Karliah traded grimaces with her. And so it went, each moment dragging on, each breath painfully long and anticipatory. They said nothing, for nothing needed to be said.

Until the door rattled.

Karliah was raising the door bar, desperate to see Konar and Appa unscathed, when Amma shot out her arm, holding it in place.

No, Amma mouthed. *Wait.* She used her eye to gesture to the outside, shaking her head as she drew Karliah's hand away.

A glare positioned itself on Karliah's face. She opened her mouth to protest when the door shook a second time, quavering under the weight of what seemed like a body slamming into it. Karliah swallowed, backed away with the knife raised before her, its lyvium blade catching the light from the lantern still perched on the map table. Appa and Konar would've called out by now. Called them by name. So would've anyone else from the crew.

An ax blade penetrated the door with a *crack,* splintering the wood. Karliah's scream scraped her throat as the weapon's wielder ripped the blade free and brought it down again, this time creating a hole that ushered in the cries of dying sailors amid the howling wind. She rushed toward Amma like a frightened hatchling and glanced back at the door just as a red-veined eye pressed against the newly created hole. It stared at her with a mixture of hatred and sadism, and Karliah understood it would mean more than death should the beholder of that eye enter. Another scream built up in her throat, ready to betray her by clawing its way out again, but before it could do so, a guttural cry tinged with rage emerged from outside the door.

Karliah's breath caught in her throat. Amma had driven one of her daggers into the would-be intruder's eye. As she pulled the bloodstained blade free, the eye came with it. Amma didn't grimace. Didn't so much as wince. Karliah halted, allowing the few feet that remained between her and Amma to ebb and flow with the weight of what had transpired. Amma knew the pain the loss of an eye brought, and according to the curve of her full lips and the thin sheen of sweat glistening on her tattooed chin, she *enjoyed* it.

"Amma?" Karliah rasped. Her knife clattered to the wooden planking beneath her feet.

Stoicism—no, passion, but controlled, ready to be used as a weapon—radiated from Amma like armor. She retrieved the knife and pressed it into Karliah's still-trembling hand, drew her close in the encompassing embrace she'd sought not moments ago.

"Shh," she breathed into Karliah's hair. "They can only hurt us if we let them."

The door cracked beneath the weight of another ax. It sounded louder, the damage more severe, as though the door were only seconds from shattering.

Karliah sunk her fingertips into the velvet of Amma's blouse, willing her eyes to look anywhere but at the door. "Will you protect me?" she whispered.

Amma guided Karliah to the left side of the door and placed herself between her daughter and their impending doom. "Always. But one day, you won't need me any longer."

An ax head ripped through the door, this time followed by a scarred arm pulling desperately at the remaining wood.

"And then what?" Karliah asked, her voice scarcely audible.

Tears pooled in Amma's sea-green eye. They did not fall. "And then I can die at peace."

A man stumbled into the room, a sword in one hand, an ax in the other. He was nearly as tall as the cabin ceiling, his head shaved and tattooed with monstrous winged creatures. He made for the cots at the opposite end of the room, but before he got there, Amma was on his back, one arm around his neck and the other plunging her dagger into his neck again and again. Blood spurted from his wounds as he dropped to his knees. The weapons fell helplessly to the floor beside him. Amma grabbed the sword and sheathed her dagger on her hip, then motioned for

Karliah to follow her out onto the deck. They had to step over the body of the red-eyed man on their way out. A sense of giddiness rippled through Karliah as she hurried after Amma, her little knife brandished in her no longer shaking hand.

Amma can do anything, she thought.

I can do anything.

The feeling soon dissipated as she ventured further into the night, the deck slick yet tacky beneath her toes as the metallic tinge of blood assaulted her nostrils. Bodies lay scattered across the ship like hut sidings after a storm. Karliah's stomach clenched as she recognized face after face of Appa's fallen crew. She'd kneeled to check the pulse of one—a young woman named Zyrah who'd taught Karliah to tie a proper knot just that afternoon—when Amma's scream rang above the storm.

Karliah squinted in the darkness, eyes widening as she took in the figure of her bretata lying on the deck with the rest of the dead. All fear abated as she leaped over the fallen bodies and joined Amma's side. Konar's mouth hung open, his head dangling limply over Amma's cradling arms. His chest, though. It still displayed the gentle rise and fall of life. Karliah swore then to all the deities that had been and all those who would ever be that she would give them anything should they allow her family to have long and happy lives.

"I can't find any wounds, save for a gash on his head," Amma said, drawing Konar closer to her bosom. "He'll be alright. He'll—"

A sound loud as thunder silenced Amma's pleas. *The Umbra* groaned in response, quivering from the impact. Members of the crew poured from the trapdoors of the lower levels like insects, and even Karliah understood what that meant.

The ship was beyond saving.

Karliah wiped the water from her eyes, little good that it did, and peered through the rain as a figure approached them. She'd nearly convinced herself she had the strength to stab whoever dared to come near her when she recognized the limp of her Appa's first mate.

"Barky!" she cried, rushing into his outstretched arms.

"Sweet girl," he murmured, stroking her head.

"Where's Appa?" Karliah drew back far enough to study the familiar creases of Barky's face, the way the lines crested his forehead like waves when he no longer bothered hiding his concern.

There was no lie in his eyes as he said, "Safe last I saw, cutting through three men for every one that dared to take a swing at him."

"Aboard *The Umbra?*" Amma called out.

The corner of Barky's mouth arced downward, but he offered a curt nod. "Aye. We both crossed back just before they severed the last of the planks. He went below to inspect the leaks."

Karliah glanced at the trapdoor, which was still spurting out members of the crew. Cold fingers curled around her heart, squeezing and pumping its rhythmic *thud* faster and louder in her ears.

Hurry, Appa.

The fact that Konar had long since outgrown his child's frame didn't stop Amma from hoisting him into a standing position, and for the first time in Karliah's short but well-trodden life, she thought she may have begun to grasp the endless bounds of a parent's love.

"How did they know?" An accusatory bite tainted Amma's speech as she shrugged off Barky's interceding hand, but her hardened gaze looked beyond the cook at the intruding ship. "I told no one our heading. Only you, me, and Kor knew."

Barky rubbed his face in the tired, exaggerated way many adults did when they didn't want to continue a conversation. "*The Umbra* is quick and sleek, but she could've been followed by any pirate worth their salt. There's only so many awskada working with the likes of us, so it be."

Amma looked ready to spew some poisonous remarks when Appa emerged from the lower deck with an expression that put the storm clouds to shame. A chunk of his hat brim was missing, and as he drew closer, Karliah made out a thin trickle of blood trailing from his collarbone to his exposed sternum. He greeted Karliah with his eyes, but she sensed his mind was with his ship. Not her. Appa may have loved her in the way other animals did their young, caring for her well-being and making sure she thrived. But his heart belonged to the sea.

Amma fixed Appa with a look every bit as sharp as a blade. "How could you leave Konar to fend for himself?"

Appa offered no excuse. He wiped his face with the soaked fabric of his sleeve as he surveyed the deck, sword light and ready in his other hand.

Another projectile struck *The Umbra*. Karliah gripped Barky's arm to keep her balance. Shivers assaulted her body, though she didn't feel cold, could hardly recognize the sting of the rain any longer.

The adults exchanged defeated looks, but it was Amma who spoke the ill-fated words.

"We must abandon ship."

Appa's response was almost a growl. "I will not."

"Then die." Amma turned to Barky and spoke with enough force to rival the storm itself. "Get the landboats. Gather your closest mates, but do so discreetly. We don't have enough..."

Amma's words faded into the gale as Karliah caught movement beyond *The Umbra*, just yonder on the horizon, behind the now retreating enemy ship. At first glance, it looked like little more than a large cloud, its dark, boundless body billowing like smoke. But clouds weren't so lengthy, so close to the water. Nor were they so tangible.

Karliah rubbed her eyes, and when she focused again, the shape was gone. Her suspicion wasn't. Amma's voice sounded like a distant dream as her bare feet slapped across the deck. When she reached the railing and allowed herself a long, shaky breath, she dared to hope that it was nothing but her imagination. The wind lashed rain against her back, prickling her arms with sharp droplets. More clouds raced across the sky like swarms of arzoks.

Just the storm, she convinced herself. *Just your wild mind.*

The other ship rocked. Not merely a rough toss from waves riled by the storm. Something beneath the ship shoved upward with enough force to raise its entire front half, tipping the enormous weapons that had assaulted *The Umbra* into the ocean. Karliah glimpsed a long, lithe body armored with thick, bristly spines splaying out into silky tips that could almost be considered beautiful, were they not larger than shark fins and attached to a body that seemed to have no beginning and no end. It slipped back beneath the waves as fast as it had appeared.

"The fuck was that?" some nameless member of the crew murmured beside her.

"Seaserpent." Her voice was a whisper, intended for her ears alone. The man beside her, oblivious to such speculation—otherwise she doubted he'd position himself so carelessly—leaned over the railing, strands of wet hair plastered to his face as he searched for what had arisen from the depths.

Old Chryia's stories swirled in Karliah's head, ones of myrem, the ancient and amphibious Vysilliam race, and the monsters they'd domesticated. It was believed the last of the Great Beasts had gone extinct following the unification of Az Zar, but the people of Zelos knew nothing in the sea ever truly died. The stormbirds and deathstalkers may have succumbed to eternal fates, but the seaserpents? They were endless. And as much as Karliah wanted to believe they were myth, she knew with a child's unshakeable certainty that was far from the truth.

More members of the crew joined Karliah at the railing. Later, she'd recall that everything changed in a matter of moments, but as she stood beside Appa's crew, saltwater stinging her eyes as they held a collective breath, it felt like an entire night had transpired in the eye of a storm. She contemplated running back to Amma, finding shelter in Appa's strong arms, but she couldn't move, didn't dare so much as flinch. If she didn't, maybe the seaserpent wouldn't sense her, wouldn't be tempted the way a predator was by fleeing prey. She tried not to imagine how large the rest of it was, given the girth and length of the tail that'd slunk back into the sea. With some pride, she restrained the scream battering against her throat.

The second time the other ship moved independently of the waves, its stern lifted from the ocean, threatening to capsize. It had scarcely regained contact with the water when it suddenly launched twenty feet into the air, the force behind the thrust tossing the ship with the ease of leaves caught in a gale. The cries of the enemy crew were drowned out by the sudden slap of the ship crashing back into the ocean, of cracking and groaning wood. Karliah's teeth chattered as a finned tail as wide as *The Umbra's* sails once again disappeared beneath the waves. She'd no pride left, but still, she restrained her scream.

The monster didn't wait long to resurface. Done with its baiting, it rose from the water, uncoiling and stretching like a wild vine until it loomed above the other ship with length to spare beneath the waves. So large it was, and the sky so dark, that it took Karliah a moment to locate its head amid the great lengths of its plated, serpentine form. Her gaze went to a glowing orb positioned above the ship. It seemed to float in the air like a spirit, emitting a gentle hum as it transitioned through a pallet of bioluminescent colors. Karliah could've stared at the orb for ages, could've fallen asleep to its rhythmic display of light. But then the seaserpent opened its eyes. Its real eyes. Located far above the orb were cooler lights, more alive, more eerie than ethereal. Large and oval. Arced downward. Black where the whites should've been. And instead of any color, just a bulge of gleaming white in the center. Eyes like the moons. Eyes that seemed to take in the entirety of its surroundings in a single glance. And they saw *The Umbra*. Saw her. She felt the gaze, cool and unwavering. Still, Karliah restrained her scream.

Two of the moons broke free from the clouds, illuminating the scene with unnerving clarity. The seaserpent arched its sinewy neck, flexing the spines that ran the length of its finned head all the way across its brow to the tip of its ridged nostrils. Its mouth opened to a trove of sharp, disorderly fangs, row upon row of varying size and placement. They were translucent and jagged, only made visible due to the brightness of the moons and their sheer size—some as large as *The Umbra's* flag. Its jaws were uneven, the bottom much longer, and from it dangled a long, glowing barbel, the thing Karliah had mistaken for an orb. Water ran down the seaserpent's shimmering black body as it hovered over the other ship. Its face showed no emotion, nor did its eyes give its intention away, but it didn't take much imagination to assume the creature took pleasure in the screams and cries rising from the other ship as it allowed them to come to terms with the severity of their situation. Now, Karliah wished desperately for her scream to free itself from her throat, to be free of the ever-building pressure.

It wouldn't come.

And the monster dove a third time.

The storm continued to abate, basking the night in a false sense of serenity as the third and final moon slithered out from beneath the clouds. The rain softened to a drizzle. The waves resumed their playful rocking. Karliah's heart fluttered inside her chest, her lips stretched thin over her teeth, the billow of her sleeve caught on a sliver of wood that wouldn't let her go—not that she cared to try, not that she'd dare to so much as flinch, not now, not when it could scent her, could pull her down into a watery grave. Not until the black jaws emerged from the water a safe distance away did she even risk so much as taking a breath. The cage of teeth yawned wide, stretching beyond the normal bounds of other creatures' jaws, and then closed around the enemy ship. With its teeth locked securely around the hull, it dragged the ship down as easily as a fish snapping up a water dancer.

It was only once the cries of the dying crew were silenced by the waves that Karliah finally screamed. A long, rasping, biting cry with enough shrillness to make her ears ring and the noise fade around her. Something wetted her pants, though she knew not if it was the fading rain or her own urine. She stumbled back into a cluster of warm bodies slick to the touch, reaching for a helping hand but securing none. Arms shoved at her, driving her back, keeping the little girl, the burden, away. The crew screamed of ghosts, of demons. Some cursed the myrem. Others cursed their gods. Tears stung Karliah's eyes as she stumbled in the direction she thought Amma waited, but she was no longer certain of anything.

She tripped over something strewn on the deck and fell face first into it. Into flesh. Into the cavern where flesh had been, her small hand caught in a crevice created by a blade, the organs inside slipping around her fingers, staining her skin with the stuff skin was supposed to keep in. She ripped her hand free and scrambled away from the body, not wanting to give it an identity, to know whose corpse she'd violated.

She couldn't help it anymore. Couldn't be brave. She screamed and screamed until her throat ached. Shut her eyes to the madness, closed her mind to the creature lurking below.

Then Appa's voice rose above the commotion, his warm baritone a beacon in the night. "Burn it down! Go below, gather all the dry wood you can find. Bring the lanterns, light the torches, ready the landboats."

Before Appa had finished speaking, a strong arm wrapped around Karliah's midsection, pulling her clam-tight fingers from her legs and carrying her back into the heart of *The Umbra*. Gerosa and Azra were already disappearing below deck, several lanterns in tow. Her captor-savior turned out to be Barky, who deposited her beside Amma and a still unconscious Konar. Amma grabbed Karliah's arm and clung to it with such intensity that she would've cried out in pain had she not desperately craved the sense of security it provided.

"I'll ready a landboat," Barky said, and vanished into the bustle of surviving crew members trampling about the ship like ants.

Amma grabbed Karliah's face and drew it closer to her own. "It's alright," she whispered. "You're safe now."

"It's coming back," Karliah said, shaking her head. "It's going to drag us down just like that other ship, going to—"

Amma clapped her hand over Karliah's mouth. "Appa is going to set the ship aflame. Seaserpents hate fire. It won't approach us. By the time it resurfaces, *The Umbra* will be roaring with heat, driving it back into the depths."

"But—"

"No." Amma glared, the fear outweighing her anger. "The landboats are small and won't draw as much attention. By the time the flame dies out, we'll find land again. The arzoks have already gone for help. Have courage, little one."

Courage evaded Karliah, but she gave Amma the confidence she sought by forcing a smile and nodding her head once for affirmation, the way Appa did after a business agreement was made. She didn't cry again either, not as heat blossomed below her feet or as sparks shot up from the trapdoor leading to the lower decks. She didn't complain as she, Barky, Azra, Gerosa, Appa, Amma, and a still unconscious Konar stole away to a special landboat, the best boat, the one with proper oars and food and drink. The one hidden inside a false wall behind Appa's cabin, the one built for crossing vast amounts of water, not for merely staying afloat like the others. Nor did she scream when Appa and his crew mates cut through their own men and women who tried to prevent their escape, tears building in their eyes as they watched the light fade from their brethren's. And as they rowed away from *The Umbra*, its masts snapping and crackling in the flames, its sails shriveling and curling until they were nothing more than ash, she didn't allow her mind to linger on what hid beneath the now tranquil waters of the Vylehk Ocean.

She did pray, however, spilling silent pleas like tears to whatever deities would listen, once again reminding them to keep her and hers safe, that she'd do anything—*anything*—should they survive what lay ahead.

Let it be content with its spoils, she said in the dark, still places of her mind, the ones unmarred by fear, the ones slowly blossoming into the adult she'd become.

Don't let it return, please.

And then, a seed of a thought, that voice again that wasn't entirely her own, the one she'd first heard beneath the floor of her family hut after Amma's ritual.

It will not return. Not until it listens to you, and you alone.

KONAR

"**Y**ou missed it, Bretata. One of the monsters from your books."

Karliah's wild eyes hooked Konar's gaze and held it as he came to on the crowded landboat, his head cradled in Amma's lap as his nostrils filled with a mixture of brine and sweat-tinged musk. His head throbbed, and a damp chill laced his skin from the still wet clothes plastered to his body. Water slapped against the side of the landboat, and above him flickered the last few stars, fighting for a chance to shine amid the graying sky. He lay there, eyelids heavy as Amma stroked his head and whispered his name in a prayer-like exhale, and he could've continued to do so had Karliah not gripped his hand with thin, sharp nails.

"Monster?" Konar mumbled, the words scraping against his throat.

Karliah glanced over her shoulder with caution. "A seaserpent," she whispered, returning her attention to him. "It ate the other ship. Dragged it down to a watery grave. It probably would've eaten *The Umbra*, too, if Appa hadn't—"

Amma silenced Karliah with a stern look.

Konar rubbed his eyes, thoughts tossing as wildly as the waves had the night prior. "A real seaserpent?" A tinge of regret sprung up in his chest and tightened his already sore throat. How come he, the researcher, the believer, the well-intended scholar, had missed out on such an amazing discovery? "How big was it? Did it have the ability to conceal itself, as the legends say? Did—"

Appa grabbed Konar's arm and jerked him to a seated position where he examined his son's body in a detached, probing manner, not unlike the techniques used by domesticators and healers. "Now is not the time for questions. Are you hurt?"

"I'm alright, Appa," Konar muttered as he threw Amma a glance to silence her incoming protests.

Appa wrinkled his nose, then returned his attention to the water. "Good. Then you're fit for rowing."

Konar found an oar in his hands before he could dispute the assignment. He moved into position beside Azra, Gerosa and Barky seated across from him, all of them glistening with sweat, the muscles on their forearms bulging as they cut through the water to an unknown destination. The nyrian and beridian regarded Konar with irritated disdain, but Barky offered one of his famous—however diluted—grins.

"Be glad you didn't lay eyes upon it, lad," Barky said, giving Konar's neck a squeeze. "Took ten years off my life just looking at it, so it did." The cook's fingers, usually warm with life (if not a bit calloused), were stiff and cool, their deftness all but non-existent.

Karliah peered doubtfully over the side of the landboat. An older, more detached presence seemed to embody her as she crawled back to the center of the boat and tucked her knees beneath her chin. "The myrem don't want us here."

"Hush, girl," Amma hissed, picking her own oar back up.

Azra glared, and Gerosa muttered something in the language of his kind, but no one hurried to tell Karliah she was a foolish girl, that the myrem didn't care, much less exist.

Konar searched the horizon for any sign of land, finding nothing but the endless expanse of ripples mirroring the silver sky. Amma and Appa's arzoks were nowhere to be found. They'd likely taken leave of *The Umbra* once things took a turn for the worse and flown straight back to Zelos to notify the contacts Appa had on standby for crises. As far as Konar knew, it was the first time executing such a plan. The first time losing a ship.

And without the arzoks' presence on the landboat, a raw sense of vulnerability engulfed him.

Konar craned his neck to distract himself with the handful of stars still dotting the sky. He could still make out the familiar ten-pointed constellation of Bongaiyo, the Amma of all stormbirds, and the guardian of the skies. There, tucked between the stars signifying her beak and the top of her head, was Elonias, the South Star. Her eye. With Elonias, any sailor worth their salt could navigate their way back from the most remote and unexplored parts of the ocean. But Appa and Amma weren't using it to guide them home. In fact—Konar gave the sky another glance—they were maintaining their distance from land, both Zelos and Az Zar, still floating around the general area Amma's vision had guided them to. Something told him they'd remain there until the scroll was found.

Appa wasn't one to return home empty-handed.

They rowed in silence until the sun reached its highest point in the sky. Its relentless rays chased away the cloud coverage, penetrating the crowded landboat with an angry heat that blistered skin and cracked lips as deeply as a dried ravine. Even Gerosa's nose, not protected by silky fur like the rest of his body, looked dry and rough to the touch. He caught Konar staring and issued a warning with a glint of his bared fangs. The lack of water and overexposure to the sun clouded Konar's senses, drowning his usual caution in a sea of frustration. He raised his oar from the water, ready to confront Gerosa with his new weapon, should it come to that, when Appa emerged from the ocean and lunged for the bow of the landboat. The vessel teetered beneath his weight as he hauled himself inside.

"What a goddesses' cursed waste," he shouted, slamming his fist against the side of the landboat with just enough self-control to keep from injuring himself. All eyes aboard the boat dodged his fiery gaze as he sought Amma's shoulders, snaring her between his strong fingers like the traps they used to keep gwanei off their property back in Zelos. "There's nothing here, Zorah. Nothing we can reach, anyhow. Was there anything else in your vision?"

Amma wrenched free of his grip. She chewed her bottom lip as she dipped her fingers in the water, combing through it, stroking it, as though she could coax the secret out of it with the right gesture. "No. This was whereabouts it showed."

"Whereabouts." Appa flung the word at her like a dagger. "Well, that's all good in principle, but legend says a human woman hid the scrolls. She couldn't have swum to the depths of the ocean to hide this one any easier than we can do now to retrieve it."

"Perhaps your vision tricked you," Barky suggested. "Or you misinterpreted it? I don't imagine assessing such things is an easy feat, no matter—"

"It wanted us to come here," Amma repeated. She shook the water from her hand. "There was something we were meant to see or do."

"Die? Get dragged to our deaths along with *The Umbra*, that we might lay eyes upon the reward just before we perish?" Appa's callous laugh sent a chill down Konar's spine.

"Maybe we couldn't bring the ship."

Konar hadn't exactly meant to join the conversation, but the nagging thought marched down from his mind and out through his mouth without warning. He pulled his book out from the confines of his shirt and held it tenderly against his chest.

"The author of this journal spent their life studying ancient times," he continued, his voice wavering slightly beneath the weight of the gazes leveled at him. "They speculated a myrem settlement is—or was—located in these waters, close to the place Amma's vision led us."

He cringed, waiting for one of Gerosa's colorful remarks, or Azra to grunt in disgust, but Appa leaned forward and said, "Go on, boy."

Konar tried his best not to stammer. "Humans and nyrians in ancient Nyzar were believed to be in communication, even community, with myrem at one point in time. Land dwellers like us wouldn't have been able to access the myrem's underwater settlements, but myrem also needed to remain close to water sources whenever they surfaced."

"They would've needed a place to suit all beings whenever gatherings were held," Amma added, following his line of thought. "And the scroll keeper would've known about such places due to the secrets of her order." She beamed at Konar, a silent exchange between them that required no words to convey her pride.

Appa unrolled the small map he kept strapped to his hip in a watertight case. "An underground cave system would need to be attached to a large landmass. Directly north of us is Az Zar's uninhabitable, rocky coastline surrounded by cliffs. It wouldn't be accessible by land, nor would a large ship be able to draw close enough safely, but..."

"But we don't have a large ship anymore," Karliah whispered. "Because we weren't supposed to. We were supposed to die, like Appa said. Just not all of us."

Konar's eyes widened as he regarded his setata, but he couldn't deny the truth of her words.

"We don't know that any such cave exists," Azra said, folding his arms across his chest.

Barky combed through an ever-whitening beard as his bushy eyebrows knitted together, wrinkling the skin above them. "Aye, we don't, but would ya rather keep diving until you drink salt water out of desperation, all the while waiting for that cursed beast to return? We need to make for land regardless, and Az Zar's southern coast is closer than Zelos."

"Then we have our heading." There was a lightness about Appa's movements as he retrieved his oar and gestured for the rest to do likewise. He even put one in Karliah's small hands, gently closing her fingers over the wood. "If we work together, we'll reach land by nightfall."

As they rowed with a sense of purpose that had too long evaded them, Konar couldn't shake the feeling that he'd altered more than their current course with his revelation.

And there was no turning back.

The cliffs appeared as the sun began its descent. Konar had never seen such a foreboding coastline, one built more like a fortress with impenetrable walls than a welcoming beach laced with silken sands. Where the shale had fallen away, the sheer faces of the cliffs were adorned in red and green stone that seemed to radiate the warm light cast by the sunset. A few seahawks had made their nests in the lips of the cliff, a home protected from predators both above and below. The land beyond the cliffs was barely visible in the fading light, but from what he could make out, it better resembled mountainous peaks than plateaus.

"Let's take her in just yonder," Appa shouted over the screeches of seahawks. They appeared to be involved in some sort of mating ritual that was as boisterous as any night at The Siren's Song. "Keep your eyes on the waterline for any shadows or signs of cutaways in the cliffside."

There were no telltale shadows in the dying light. No gaping cave mouths. No hints of cutaways leading to mysterious caverns beneath the water. They rowed alongside the cliffs until Konar's arms, long since exhausted by the journey, all but gave out, only capable of one quivering row for every five the elder men completed. Exhaustion hadn't spared them, though. It was evident in Barky's fixed frown, in Azra's clenched jaw, in the way Gerosa's claws flexed out to graze the handle, each pass digging deeper into the wood. Even Appa and Amma wore defeat in the puffy bags beneath their eyes. Konar touched the sensitive skin beneath his own eyes, wondering if he too bore signs of fatigue. Karliah had taken it a step further and emitted gentle snores, curled up beside Amma's feet like a cat. By the time Appa ordered them to turn back (they'd gone far beyond the coordinates in Amma's vision), a chill cut through the night air, made worse by Konar's newly acquired fever. It blurred his vision and set his teeth to an endless chatter.

"We have to call it off, Korandon," Amma pleaded as she rowed. "The children can't go much longer without water. Konar's stricken with fever, and Karliah—"

"Then they shouldn't have come!" Appa snapped. He rowed faster, as if reinvigorated by Amma's suggestion.

Barky's eyebrows raised, but he didn't dare interject himself into his captain's affairs. He knew better than most that Appa resisted any voice not his own.

Konar faded in and out of consciousness, losing all sense of time. When Appa finally slowed his efforts long enough to bring an open palm to Konar's forehead, he startled, realizing he'd fallen asleep on his oar.

"Your amma said this was all too good to be true," Appa muttered, wincing as his hand registered the heat Konar's head emitted. "Always right, aren't you?" That question he directed at Amma, but she didn't grace him with a reply. Only a narrowed eye directed at the cliff side. Appa gave Konar's back a firm pat, the closest he ever came to a hug, and groaned in resignation. "There's a port half a day's row from here. If we work through the night—"

Gerosa's roar drowned out both the seahawks and Appa alike as he stood in the boat, ears pinned back and tail flicking with anticipation. He pointed at a place where two exceptionally tall rock spires conjoined.

Only they didn't. Not quite.

Konar narrowed his eyes as Appa and the crew rowed vigorously toward the dark shadow beneath, toward a small tunnel so glaringly obvious now it was a wonder they hadn't seen it before. Unless...

"Low tide!" Barky shrieked, at least as much as a man his age with a voice as deep as the sea could. He loosed a hearty laugh that made Konar smile despite his fever.

Amma stood, oar planted beside her like a spear, and regarded Barky with stern anticipation. "Improper interpretation of my vision, was it?"

"My lady," Barky said, wiping a stray tear from his eye brought upon by his laughter. "Let me be the first to swear I'll never doubt you again."

"Let's save our swearing for when we've located the loot," Appa grumbled. "This isn't over yet."

They skirted the rocks jutting around the cave entrance like guardians, dodging the sharp edges with ease as the landboat slipped into the narrow space perfectly suited for a vessel of its size. No longer needed, oars were drawn into the boat and tucked beneath the bench seats. Karliah sat up in a groggy stupor, eyes half closed and lips parted lazily as she took in her surroundings. Konar's fever, no less severe than it had been moments before, fell into the back of his consciousness as he took in the sights before him. The cave walls rippled with the reflection of the moonlight cast upon the water, creating an ethereal atmosphere that both calmed and awakened him. Ahead, it narrowed into a dark tunnel dusted with the barest hint of a light blue glow. Rock walls closed around the landboat, so tightly that Konar could reach up and stroke the slick, cool texture of the rock above him, then tighter still, forcing him to press against the others like grubs in a fishing sack. The walls brightened the further they drifted, giving way from a black-blue to a graying blue light, and finally, as the tunnel widened again, they basked in a cool color not unlike starlight.

Konar bolted upright as soon as there was room to do so, pushing over Gerosa and stepping on Azra's shoulder as he made his way to the front of the boat. They'd floated into the mouth of a cave as large as Tongura's village center and as tall as the awskada's towering fortress. Dangling from the ceiling were hundreds—maybe thousands—of luminescent strings emitting the blueish-white light that illuminated the rock walls and stalactites. At first, he took the light sources for minerals, like the much-coveted nevethium crystals. But as he studied them closer, he caught one moving, ever so slightly, and noted the soft, gelatin texture coating their long, boneless bodies.

Not entirely unlike the tentacles of anemones, he mused, stretching his hand out directly below one. He couldn't actually touch it; the closest one was a good spear's length away, but he reached for it just the same.

No one aboard the landboat uttered a sound. The surroundings commanded the same reverence from the rest of the crew as it did from Konar, as though all had come to a similar conclusion: the cave was sacred. Not in the way of the Mavist temples sprouting up all over Zelos at the command of the emperor. Those were forced, sterile. Demanding and cold. Ceremonial.

The cave, however, commanded respect and reflection, the way the sea did when one stared off at its vast expanse of life-giving power. Or the way one could only stand in awe before a tree that had long outlived generations of nyrians, or how touching certain stones bespoke the secrets of time itself. How, when one gazed into the eyes of a dying kill or a recently harvested plant, a moment of understanding was exchanged.

Yes, the cave such held secrets, and Konar wanted nothing more than to spend an eternity uncovering them all.

"Bit dramatic, hiding a magical artifact in a hidden cave with glowing ceiling dangles," Barky mused, shattering Konar's dream with a reminder of why they'd really come. "Believable, though. I bet you all my secret kelp recipe it's here."

Appa ignored him. "Pull in over there."

Konar followed Appa's outstretched finger to where the water met a smooth ramp of rock leading up to dry ground. A few feet inland sat something akin to a giant, circular bench with no backrests. At least fifty adults of good size could've taken a seat after entering through the one gap in the otherwise unbroken loop. It looked so natural, so organic in form, that he almost believed it wasn't brought forth by the hands of another being long ago.

Or maybe it was. Maybe it was all the same, the care genuine, the process intentional, whether by mortal, deity, or the land itself.

They got out where the water ran shallow and dragged the landboat onto the rocky surface. Karliah scampered off, making excited little squeals as she scooped up small pebbles and traced them through luminescent puddles; puddles Konar quickly determined as the hanging glow creatures' excrement. Amma gave Appa and the rest of the crew the look of a mother relishing her divine rightness, almost daring them to question her judgement again.

"A gathering hall fit for the elite," Gerosa said as he stretched his massive frame out directly atop the rocky ground in the middle of the circle. "And nowhere to keep things hidden."

"Probably still underwater," Azra shouted from across the cave, where he'd disappeared behind a mountain of stalagmites. "I've found at least two waterways that appear to lead to underground cave systems."

"How deep can you see?" Appa asked, wringing out a puddle from his patched socks.

There was silence for a moment, followed by a splash. A few moments later, another splashing sound, then Azra's voice: "Can't see shit. Didn't so much as touch rock the whole time."

Appa and Barky groaned, and Gerosa's whiskers offered the slightest twitch.

Amma gave a knowing smile as she shook her head. "The scroll keeper was human. It must be somewhere in the surface tunnels. If we can't access it, then she couldn't have, either."

"Unless she had myrem acquaintances," Barky countered. "Someone willing to stow it for her."

Gerosa flashed a yawn that looked as relaxed as it did intimidating. "I'll hack this cave apart rock by rock if it's standing between me and my aspar."

Konar didn't doubt for a moment the beridian would. He spread out with the others, searching every crevice and cutaway for signs of a secret passageway, or perhaps some hidden compartment, like the one on *The Umbra* that kept the landboat away from greedy eyes. He traced his boot through piles of goo. Jiggled loose rocks. Stuck his hand in dark crevices. Ran the expanse of the cave with Karliah and Appa until they'd followed all routes to where they dead ended or descended into black depths below.

It didn't take long for Konar's fever to resurface with a vengeance. He found himself curled up in a ball, wetted by both the damp of the rock and the sweat from his skin, as footsteps reverberated off the cave walls around him. The search continued for at least half the night while he lay there, cheek cool, forehead burning. Barky knelt beside him once, offering the last of his personal waterskin, and Konar deemed it the sole reason he finally broke his fever a few hours later. If it was even that long. There was no proper sense of time passing in the cave, not with the only light source being the luminescent creatures hanging above.

When he awoke, no one was within his line of sight from where he rested near the landboat, but the voices echoing around him confirmed they weren't too far ahead, exploring the tunnels. He tried to sit up, wincing at the pain. The fever left his bones achy and his head light. He struggled to his feet and took a few shaky steps before grabbing onto the nearest rock face for support.

When it shifted beneath his fingers, not once, but continuously, Konar could've assumed he'd dislodged loose pieces of stone.

When it seemed to change form before his eyes, sprouting definable limbs in the same tone and texture of the rock, he could've explained it as post-fever delirium.

But when it spoke, well.

He could summon no logical explanation.

"Why have you awakened me?" the rock groaned.

Its voice was ancient, filled with dust and creaks, and loud enough to fill the immediate caves and beyond. Slowly, the rock shifted and shook, sending a wave of dust and crumbling pebbles to the ground. Stone fingers covered in barnacles clenched and unclenched. A head defined by sharp edges of rock mixed with wavey sections of fossilized shells took shape atop scalloped shoulders. Thick legs appeared, at first seated, then rising to stand, exposing bits of stringy muscle and flesh in the gaping holes of the otherwise stone and shell frame.

Now standing, the creature towered over Konar, easily dwarfing even Gerosa's lofty height. A line formed on its head, revealing a toothless black cavern he assumed must be its mouth. Then a single, dreadful eye appeared above a fleshy cavity in its cheek. A cold, lidless eye the color of smoke. It had no pupil, but Konar felt it watching him all the same, tracking his every movement. Every breath. The creature took a step toward him, a step that was more of a drag. Its foot never fully detached from the stone ground, just slid through it as though it offered no more resistance than water.

A scream lodged in Konar's throat.

"Waste not my time, for your sake," the creature bellowed, sliding its left foot to meet the right.

Konar staggered back, his hands fanning out behind him just in time to brace his fall. The creature slid forward until it stood directly over him. Cool water trickled from its exposed cavities, sliding down its rock body and pooling on the ground beneath. A few drops collected on the creature's chin and landed on Konar's cheek. One found its way into his still gaping mouth.

Saltwater.

"Touch him, and I'll throw your body into the sea piece by piece."

A sense of calm eased back into Konar at the sound of Amma's voice. He dared a glance over his shoulder and saw her standing a few feet behind him, Karliah on her left, Appa on her right. Behind them stood Barky, Azra, and Gerosa. All glaring. All armed.

Appa put a hand on Amma's shoulder to silence whatever hostile comment she readied. "Are you the guardian of this cave?" he asked, lowering his sword to kiss the ground. "We've come to—"

"I know why your kind comes." The rock creature moved its eye to study Appa with what appeared to be great effort. "You come when you have need, and you abandon us when you need not."

A dagger grazed the creature's head, chipping away a fleck of rock. Konar recognized the lyvium blade as Gerosa's, one he'd won in a bet moons past. The creature's cold eye narrowed, slowly tracing its gaze from the fallen dagger to the beridian.

"You are not welcome here," said the voice rumbling from its core. Konar noted that although it had the semblance of a mouth, the source of its speech came from deeper within.

Gerosa crept forward, claws flexed, Azra on his tail.

The rock creature roared until the walls of the cave shivered and the ground beneath Konar trembled. A few of the glowing creatures came loose from the ceiling and fell to the ground, their flexible bodies remaining fully intact despite the extreme impact.

"We've gone to great lengths to arrive here," Appa said, his voice steady despite the wildness in his eyes. "I've sacrificed much."

"It matters not," the rock creature rumbled. Something akin to pity carved into its features before hardening back to its callous scowl. "You will not find what you seek here."

"I know it's here, Guardian." Amma pulled her hand free from Karliah's and kneeled before the rock creature. "It called to me."

The rock creature said nothing to this. The ground beneath Konar quavered in an uncertain sort of way, not as though it intentionally wanted to crack the barrier and plunge him into a watery prison below.

"I am not its guardian," the creature said. "Though I have resigned myself to such duties for endless moons." It groaned as its limbs lengthened in formations not unlike the cliffs outside. This show of size and strength halted Gerosa from where he slunk forward in the shadows. "And though it may have called you here, as others before you have claimed, it still has not chosen you, awskada. Unworthy." The corners of his cavernous mouth turned down. "Unworthy. Unworthy. Unworthy."

"I'll show 'im who's worthy," Azra said, leaping forward with his sword raised above his head. He slammed his blade down on the rock creature's neck with a resounding *clang*, denting the metal with a jolt that loosened his grip.

The cave shook again, this time causing several of the smaller formations to topple. A few stalactites broke free from above and pierced the ground with hundreds of fragmented shards upon impact. One barely missed Appa. Konar remained rooted to the place he'd fallen, not daring to upset the creature further.

A large, salt-stained hand raised before them in warning. "Bring the cave down, and I will remain. My kind always do."

"Spirit walker," Amma said, as if the name had come to her suddenly, an awareness of what—who—it was.

Konar would've slapped his own forehead had he not been so terrified. He'd read about such beings. Life sprung from the very womb of nature herself. Beings not bound to one shape or lifetime, instead arising when and where needed from the organic materials around them. Some believed they were of the gods, others believed they were the gods themselves. Konar believed them more as a manifestation of respect for the natural world. A symbol.

Until now.

When the creature didn't deny the title Amma had assigned it, she crawled closer to it. To Konar. "You must be weary of your duty. Please, let us ease the burden. I swear to my Amma's Amma it will remain in good hands."

The spirit walker seemed to consider this. Who knew how long it had waited in the bowels of a long-forgotten cave with nothing but mournful winds and luminous worms to keep it company?

Finally, it straightened itself to near-statue form and said, "You cannot ensure that any more than you can ensure you will leave this cave alive." Amma opened her mouth to object, but the spirit walker silenced her with a rumble. "Yet, I sense a presence, one not yet tarnished by self-preservation."

It closed its eye and raised a hand to the center of its torso, then pressed there with delicate force. The rock of its chest gave to that of its fingers, absorbing them one by one until its entire hand disappeared inside, barnacles and all.

"Yes. There is one here who is worthy." The spirit walker started to pull its hand free, then halted. "She said it would know. That it would recognize the one necessary to fulfill its purpose." Another groan filled the cave as the spirit walker lowered its barrel-sized head to Konar's own. He tried to still the fear coiling in his chest as he forced his gaze to meet the spirit walker's. "Though I sense evil on your path, it is not for me to decide whether it spawns from you or is merely drawn to you."

Konar's throat tightened. The tension in the cave was thick as a sailing rope, secured around him and pulling, pulling. He should've stayed home, should've never offered the knowledge that led them to the cave, should've never touched the rock that came to life.

But something meant for him to. Destined, like Amma. And this would make Appa proud, surely.

He extended a trembling hand toward the spirit walker and awaited the item that would change his life forever.

Because even then, he knew it would.

KARLIAH

K arliah never got a good look at the scroll, and not for a lack of exhausting every resource available to her. Its brine-crusted case had only sat in her bretata's hand for a few moments before Appa was whisking them away, back to the landboat and out from the watchful, other-worldly gaze of the rock-monster guardian. Then it disappeared into a secret pocket inside Appa's water-resistant coat and remained there the rest of the voyage home.

Hiding it did little to make the others ignorant of its presence. Even though Appa forbade everyone from speaking of it until they were safely returned to Zelos, the surviving crew mates exchanged greedy looks reserved for the distribution of loot at the end of a job. Amma and Appa, however, pretended it didn't exist and told the captain of *The Deathdrop* as much when it arrived, guided by arzoks, to rescue *The Umbra's* survivors.

"Mighty loyal creatures to have at your disposal," *The Deathdrop's* captain said as her crew hauled their landboat aboard. She was a stocky nyrian with a lyvium ring pierced through her septum and eyes as vibrant as the magenta tentacles of the plant she'd named her ship after. She jutted a cleft chin toward Amma's vanishing arzok. "I tried to secure one when I came of age, but none of them would have me. Wasn't the last time I was rejected either."

Barky forced a laugh at the captain's self-deprecating comment, but the rest of the crew offered little more than exhausted smiles. Appa's arzok flashed her fangs before disappearing into the horizon after Amma's. They'd be home when the Brunes arrived, no doubt waiting for a reward.

"I'll pay you double for our fare," Appa said once they were settled with blankets and skins of water. Amma had taken Konar below deck to see to his fever, but Karliah opted to stay above where the air wasn't suffocated by the stench of countless unwashed bodies.

The captain—Karliah had seen the woman a handful of times but never taken the care to commit her name to memory—offered Appa a drink from a leather-wrapped bottle strapped to her hip. It smelled like kolaash, and to Karliah's surprise, Appa took a polite sip. The glances exchanged between her and Appa made Karliah's stomach roil.

"Sorry for your loss," the captain said, taking another swig before she passed the bottle to a grateful Azra. "Was a good ship, *The Umbra*. Will the emperor cover any expenses? You lost her in service to him, after all."

Appa's lips thinned as he shook his head. "He didn't hold a dagger to my throat to take on the cursed job, and he won't clean up my mess when it benefits him not. I took a risk for a reward that could change my life. And so it has."

"So it has," the captain said, squeezing his shoulder. "You'll be back to terrorize the sea in no time, Brineheart. Can't nothing hold you down for long."

Barky gave Karliah a roll of his eyes as the two captains walked toward the helm, shoulder to shoulder, private words shared between them. He held a finger to his lips, then joined Azra and Gerosa at the railing. They'd taken to finishing the rest of the captain's kolaash, probably happy, for once, to not be the ones responsible for the ship's wellbeing.

As the sun crested the waters and warmed the deck with its golden heat, Karliah couldn't shake the chill coursing through her like a current. She reached into her pocket and squeezed her doll for comfort, twisting the lengths of its leather-strand hairs about her fingers. Amma and Appa intended to keep the scroll hidden—that much she knew. But to do what with it? Bury it in some dark cave on Zelos, this time without a guardian, to await the next treasure hunter clever enough to track its path? Even if they did just that, Karliah wasn't certain the scroll would comply. It had an energy about it, as though it understood its purpose as much as any other being, and if she sensed it that strongly, who was to say others wouldn't?

Secure it, that voice inside her whispered, the one she'd come to know almost well enough to be her own, as though some future version of herself guided her path. *They mustn't have it. Only you.*

Karliah found an isolated place in between supply barrels and lay there, pulling the blanket she'd been given over her head to shroud her body in darkness. As soon as she shut her eyes, visions of the scroll's salt-crusted case danced in her mind, but now glowed and pulsed with the rhythm of a heartbeat.

"Only me," she whispered as she drifted off into a troubled sleep.

Only me.

They'd been home safe for a moon cycle when Karliah took what was rightfully hers. Appa and Amma had ceased all discussion of the scroll, told the surviving crew to forget it existed and that they'd pay them for their efforts in time, and both had taken up local jobs to save for said payments and a new ship. Amma tended tables at The Siren's Song, and Appa worked long hours harvesting bugana and from it crafting yasaakas to sell in the marketplace. The latter amused Konar, who knew of Appa's deep hatred for the small boats, but he'd stopped laughing soon after Appa apprenticed him to the craft.

Karliah helped where she could, harvesting wild herbs and taking care of the hut chores and cooking when the rest of the family worked long hours. And though they labored without complaint, it wasn't sustainable. Not for the Brunes, who craved adventure and freedom, variety and spontaneity—not the shackles of everyday living.

And the scroll could solve their problems, Karliah knew. They all must've known, but no one spoke of it. No one had even bothered to crack open its case and dared to read whatever was transcribed on its ancient parchment.

Maybe it isn't even made of parchment, Karliah wondered one night as she fell asleep to Konar's heavy breathing and the sound of Amma and Appa's heated discussion drifting beneath the door. *Maybe it's invisible, only revealing itself to the right person. Maybe I'm that person, the way Konar was the right one to receive it in the first place.*

Or maybe there's nothing in there at all.

That much wasn't true, though. It couldn't be. Something alive was nestled within that case. Something with the power to change her life. And she wasn't going to wait around any longer to find out.

Not long before dawn, Karliah slipped from her cot and padded barefoot to the door of the room she shared with Konar. Amma and Appa had long since quieted, but she still opened it with the utmost care. The room without was dark, but not dark enough to impair her nyrian vision, especially when she'd spent the past few hours staring at the darker nothingness of her own room.

Amma was nowhere to be found, likely snoring away in her cot in some kolaash-induced stupor, but a figure was crumpled over the table, buttocks still planted in the chair. No sound came from the sleeping man, but if Karliah had applied the correct amount of sleepstalk to Appa's pipe weed, he wouldn't stir. She'd been cautious in her distribution: too much of the root resulted in a sleep one never woke from, but too little wouldn't produce more than a slight calming effect. Thankfully, it hadn't taken much aspar to convince old Chryia to spill what she knew about the plant, including doses and where best to find it. When Karliah had harvested it from the jungle surrounding her family hut, humming to herself with a deep sense of satisfaction usually reserved for taking advantage of Az Zarian highborns, she decided that maybe she would make a fine awskada herself, given the chance.

A pinprick of guilt pierced her heart as she watched her appa asleep on the table, though. Dead to the world. But would he not hesitate to do the same to her if he felt it best for the family?

He'd do it even if it was only the best for him, and him alone.

The thought, this one undeniably her own, startled her with its rawness and truth. She shook her head to silence it and stole over the chair where Appa slept. He'd fallen asleep with his coat on, something he'd taken to doing ever since he'd tucked the scroll inside.

Karliah's hand was calm and controlled as she slipped it through the opening, pausing for a moment to judge the effectiveness of his dosage. When Appa's breathing didn't change, she probed further, fingers trailing the worn velvet lining until they located the hidden pocket inside. The scroll case seemed to come alive at her touch. She lingered for a moment, not wanting to disrupt whatever connection she'd fostered, but then Appa let out a long moan, one alarming enough that Karliah didn't want to wait around to see how soon he'd wake. The scroll slid free of its confines, and she skittered away into the night, her loot tucked beneath her armpit like it was a part of her. Like it'd always belonged there.

Belonged to her.

She didn't dare open it with her family hut in sight, nor did she feel comfortable in the obscurity of the jungle. She ran until the leaves came alive with the first pink highlights of dawn, until the serpents slithered back into the branches, until the sirens ceased their lullabies. She ran further still, up to the base of the arzok mountain, where a slight deviation in the rock gave way to soft dirt, and that dirt to a tunnel only large enough for a child to crawl through.

Even I won't fit in here much longer, she mused as she scooted along on her belly, the sharp rocks protruding from the ground digging into her elbows.

Darkness engulfed the tunnel by the time she reached the place where she could continue no further because of her size, even if the passage went on for ages. The ground was too rocky to dig in, so she pressed the scroll into a small cutaway and covered it with loose stones.

"I'll be back tonight," she whispered, patting the exposed edge of the case. "I promise."

It was only unerring confidence in her hiding place that allowed Karliah to slowly inch back out of the tunnel, away from what she already felt would be the dearest possession she'd ever own. No one knew of her special spot, not even her bretata.

Sunlight streamed through the trees like ethereal spears as Karliah skittered back into the clearing of her family hut. She raced across the still dewy ground and tiptoed up the stairs, pausing at the door to listen. The hut was silent, as she'd expected. The sleepstalk would've hindered Appa's usual early rising habits, and Amma rarely woke early since taking on the evening shifts. Konar was the only one she was uncertain about, but even if he caught her creeping back in, surely she could talk her way out of it. Or get him to keep the secret until she had a chance to read the scroll later that night.

A silent giggle bloomed in Karliah's throat as she eased the latch open. It never got the chance to bubble out.

As the door groaned open, her gaze went to where Appa was seated, where Appa *should've* been seated, and found the space empty. Her heartbeat quickened, and she backed up instinctively, ready to flee until she'd prepared a better story about where she'd been and why. She'd taken no more than two steps when she backed into something that was far too malleable to be a door. A rough, fish scented hand clamped over her mouth, pressing her into a bulky form she instantly deemed dangerous. She squirmed and kicked, but the intruder held her tight.

A searing cackle of a laugh filled the room. The hairs on Karliah's neck prickled as a wisp of a nyrian stalked out from the shadows, half his moon white hair pulled up from his face in a sleek braid that trailed halfway down his back. His cheeks were hollow, his skin so pallid that Karliah would've mistaken him for dead was he not studying her with blazing eyes.

"This is the last one?" he asked in Zarith, and Karliah was thankful—not for the first time—that Appa and Amma had seen to it she and Konar spoke both Zarith and Nyrinian alongside their native Zelosi tongue.

The man holding her grunted and shoved her closer to the Az Zarian highborn with the dead skin.

"What a shame to involve children so young in such obscene crimes," the highborn said as he looked down at Karliah with a mixture of pity and disgust. "This girl can't be more than six."

Karliah could almost hear Appa saying, *yes, let them think you're younger than you are,* so she held her tongue and let the man think just that. She even lowered her gaze and sniffled a little for good measure.

The highborn made *tsk tsk* sounds with his tongue, then said, "Let's reunite the family, shall we?"

The door to Karliah's room creaked open. Masked figures swathed head to toe in black—the types of men she'd seen escorting Az Zarian highborns on their leisure trips to Zelos—emerged, leading Appa, Amma, and Konar. Thick rope secured each of her family member's hands behind their backs, and Amma and Appa were also gagged with strips of cloth. Blood trickled from the corner of Appa's mouth, staining the white cloth crimson. Amma's eye filled with tears threatening to spill over. But Konar leveled her with a knowing look, one that seemed both angry and accusatory at once.

Guilt seized Karliah tighter than the hands holding her hostage, the ones pressing into her tender flesh and leaving the beginnings of bruises. These men had come for the scroll, and it was her fault her family wasn't prepared for them.

The frail highborn jutted a spindly thumb in Appa's direction. "Remove his gag."

One of the masked men ripped the cloth free from Appa's mouth. When Appa didn't speak immediately, the man brought a fist down on Appa's cheek, hard enough that Appa took a knee to keep from losing his balance. Karliah's jaw clenched as Appa spat out a blood-soaked tooth.

But she didn't cry out.

The highborn made his way to Appa's side, opposite the blood puddle. "Where is it, Brineheart?"

Appa shrugged, his violet eyes so intense that the pink flecks in the inner ring nearest his pupils seemed to burn. "Your guess is as good as mine."

The masked man holding Appa looked to the highborn, who nodded. A fist connected with Appa's stomach, and he doubled over in silent pain.

"I'll give you one more chance." An irritated boredom drenched the highborn's voice, as though he were haggling prices with a merchant in the village center.

A chill spread from Karliah's hands, up her arms, down her neck, back, sides.

Say something, Appa.

The highborn's hands flew up in exasperation. "We know you have it, so don't waste my time with another story about a mythical attack from a seaserpent." He squatted beside Appa so he could look him directly in the eyes; a simple act that proved to be extremely challenging for a man not used to lowering himself. "I wouldn't be surprised if you hid your ship on some foreign shore as a way to squeeze extra aspar from our already dwindling coin purses."

Appa snorted at that, and Karliah found a similar sentiment painted on Amma's face. She shouted something muffled by the gag, and the highborn flicked his hand at her captor, giving him permission to remove it.

"We lost all but three members of our crew," Amma spat as soon as the gag came off. "I almost lost..." Emotion choked her words, and Karliah had to withdraw her gaze from her amma's face. "We gave everything for nothing. Please, let us be."

The highborn seemed to consider this, perhaps as moved by Amma's performance as Karliah. He stalked toward Amma like a hunter approaching its prey, his hands clasped behind his back. Amma flinched as he reached a sharp fingernail to her face and traced it delicately around her eye patch, all while a poisonous smile creeped across his cheeks.

"I want to believe you. Really, I do." The highborn snaked his hands back into the swaths of his sleeves. The silk was a vibrant red, and the sleeves and hem of his robe trailed all the way to the floor. "There's just this one nagging detail I can't seem to shake." He broke away from Amma and clapped his hands. "Let's hurry this along, shall we?"

Karliah's captor moved her from the doorway to the center of the room, a few feet away from Konar. He only held onto her wrist, but it was enough to keep her hostage. It may as well have been a lyvium cuff clamped around her arm. She could kick him *there*, the way Appa had shown her. It would weaken the strongest of men, at least for a moment. But there was no way to warn her family, and if she fled now, what help could she be to them?

A shadow appeared in the sunlight streaming in through the doorway. Karliah recognized something familiar in the figure's gate as it approached, the way one leg seemed to drag behind the other. And as her heart pleaded no, tried to distract her with the potential of it being any number of people, her mind began drawing conclusions and acknowledging the indisputable facts.

Appa had sent a tuross as soon as they arrived home, stating their withdrawal from the mission due to the loss of their ship and crew. The emperor would've sent people immediately if he'd any reason to disbelieve Appa's claim, not waited a full moon cycle. Someone else had contacted Az Zar, someone not in the

Brune family because Karliah didn't for a moment doubt the loyalty of Amma or Konar.

And that only left three people, two of whom wouldn't act without the approval of their leader, a man she'd come to love almost as much as her own appa.

Tears blurred Karliah's vision as she took in the man who'd been there for her arrival aboard *The Umbra*, been there for Appa's arrival, the man who'd taught her not only how to catch a fish but how to cook it, the only man she'd ever felt safe with outside her true kin.

Barky wasn't looking at her, wasn't looking anywhere, really. His eyes were glazed over as though he'd withdrawn into his own protective world, one where pursuing his life's dream made it alright to betray the closest people he had to family. He raised an unbound hand to rub his nose, then dropped it to his side again, lifeless.

Rage swirled inside Karliah, making quick work of the already fading sadness. She glared at his silver-white hair, a trait humans only acquired when they lived to be a certain age, a way for them to taste the wisdom that came with it, wisdom they could never fully put to use in their fleeting lifespans. The worst part was that it all made sense. Barky was too close to the end of his life to care about anyone but himself, too near to tasting his own mortality to make any more sacrifices that didn't result in his immediate benefit. When Appa took away his last chance at a life of luxury, it must've been enough to justify...

No. She struggled against her captor's grip, a low growl rumbling in her throat. He'd been waiting his whole life for the perfect opportunity, and finally, he'd found it.

"Come in, come in," the highborn said, gesturing to where they'd all gathered at the center of the room, around the family table, of all places. Barky took a few steps inside, but kept his distance. "The nagging detail," the highborn continued, "is that this man says you have it. Preposterous, I know, but I'm almost inclined to believe him as he swears to have been present when it was"—he directed his attention to Barky—"how did you say it? Pulled from the heart of a living rock monster?" When Barky didn't so much as raise his head to acknowledge the accusation, the highborn sighed and draped his arm across Appa's shoulders. "No matter. I have three witnesses who swear you found it against three who swear you didn't, two of which are children, your blood, and wholly unreliable in that regard. And the other an awskada?" He *tsked* again. "I'm sure you can understand which story I'm inclined to believe."

"You're a spineless, shell-sucking human," Appa said. His gaze was low, his voice cool and collected, but there was no mistaking the revulsion in it or who he directed the comment at. "And you're dead to me. You and all your kind."

Barky shuffled his weight from one foot to the other, his face angled down to hide any emotion.

The highborn cleared his throat. "Heartfelt words, I'm sure." He raised Appa's chin, and for a moment Karliah feared he'd bite off the highborn's fingers, sealing their fates. But Appa maintained his restraint. "This is your last chance to tell me where you've hidden the scroll. You won't receive any reward for it, nor any reimbursement for your losses; however, the emperor is prepared to offer you the exchange of your family's lives, provided you all remain respectable citizens and cease all piracy effective immediately."

Karliah almost spoke then. Anything was worth her life and her family's, even the one thing that could make their lives better. For what were all the glories of Quorath worth with no one left to share them with? But as she opened her mouth, Appa shot her a silencing look, one that communicated he knew she'd taken it, and to keep it a secret. A look that said he didn't want the scroll to become a weapon in the hands of Barky or the emperor, no matter the cost. She looked to Amma and Konar. Amma refused to meet her gaze and sealed her lips in a tight line, the corners of her brows bunching together. Only Konar seemed uncertain, but he didn't offer her aid in the form of a disproving or encouraging look.

It was death for them all, then. A single tear trailed down Karliah's cheek.

"Now, Brineheart, or I'll rip your family apart piece by piece while you look on." A deep purple flushed the highborn's cheeks and forehead as he turned to Barky, fuming. "You're his first mate, are you not? Where would he place an item of great value?"

Barky only shrugged. "He'd never tell me. He never has."

"Fine." The highborn snatched Karliah's arm with such unexpected vigor that she found herself off-balance and stumbling toward the door with him. "I'll start with this one."

Karliah was only half surprised to see Azra and Gerosa waiting outside. The former leaned against the railing of their deck, arms crossed in front of him as he looked up at the sky in some forced attempt to busy himself with the weather. The tension in his clean-shaven jawline was the only hint that he wanted to appear more at ease than he was. Gerosa, however, met Karliah's gaze with unabashed intensity. His tail flicked back and forth with the twitchy agitation of a viper, and his claws slowly extended and retracted with practiced ease. Karliah glared at him through her tears. She'd get them back for this. All of them.

And she'd never trust an outsider again.

The highborn shoved her toward Gerosa, then wiped his hands on his robes once he was free of her. His men dragged the rest of her family outside. Karliah tried to join them where they'd lined up against the hut siding, but as soon as she dared a step, the beridian snatched her up by the back of her tunic and dangled her over the railing. A sick, light sensation filled her stomach as her bare feet squirmed in mid-air. It was a good thirty feet to the ground, and the dirt beneath the hut was hard-packed.

You can survive it, she told herself. *Tuck and roll.*

That hope went out like a candle as Gerosa extended a single claw with his free hand and held it inches from her throat.

"No!" Amma screamed. "She's just a child. We would never tell her anything." Tears dripped down her cheek and onto the deck.

The highborn rubbed his eyes and yawned, then raised his hand as if ready to give Gerosa leave to carry out Karliah's execution. "Your allies say otherwise." He returned his attention to Appa. "Last chance, Brineheart. Where is the scroll?"

"Just tell them where it is!" Konar shouted. "Tell them, Karliah! Tell them!" Appa bared his teeth to silence Konar's outburst, but her bretata didn't so much as glance his way. His eyes, wide and pleading, showed far more concern than either of her parents.

She shut her own.

"The boy fears for his setata," she heard Appa shouting over Konar's incessant pleas. "He'll say anything to protect her, but it doesn't change the fact that we've never touched your cursed scroll and never will."

Karliah opened her eyes in time to see the highborn giving Gerosa the nod that would end her life. She swallowed, bracing herself for what she hoped would at least be a painless—

"Time's up," Gerosa hissed. "Now you'll pay for your brother's big mouth that landed me in prison for endless moon cycles. Do you have any idea how they treat beridians in Az Zarian prisons?" He bared his fangs. "What's about to happen to you will be a mercy compared to it, really."

Karliah's resolve slipped away like sand through her fingers. She writhed and screamed, clawing at Gerosa's unrelenting grip with all the force she could muster. Her ears rang with her own shouts and those of her family. It was enough to loosen Gerosa's grip, but then she was falling, falling...

I love you, Konar. It was the last thought in her mind as her limbs splayed out before her, bracing for impact. A single sob rattled her throat.

A sudden jolt seized her body, but no pain accompanied it. Only the wind tugging at her hair and sending prickles up and down her exposed legs and arms. She didn't want to open her eyes, didn't want to take the chance that this was actually death, not some miracle moment where she'd learned to fly. But then her feet touched ground, and the clawed toes she hadn't been aware were holding her released her upper arms, freeing her of the illusion of weightlessness.

A shadow covered Karliah, then drifted to the space beyond her as a shriek filled the air. She looked up just in time to see Amma's arzok careening toward the deck, claws spread, fangs bared, his mate mere seconds behind him. Gerosa swiped at him, but Amma's arzok was ready and altered his course enough to dodge the beridian, but not so much as to avoid snagging him with a stray claw, yanking him over the railing. The beridian roared as he fell, but quickly controlled his descent. He landed unharmed, as only his kind could do, then located Karliah with narrowed eyes.

Karliah's heart thudded in her ears as she tried to regain command of her body. Her legs worked into a mindless run, but not before Gerosa was on her. Searing pain ripped across her back as she fell, then she was on her belly, face in the dirt, its sweet musk filling her nostrils. She whimpered, waiting.

No further attack came.

She pressed herself up, wincing as fresh, throbbing pain radiated through the skin of her back. Gerosa lay sprawled in the dirt behind her, a dagger plunged into his head. Blood matted in his fur, staining his golden coat red. He didn't stir. Behind him stood Konar, mouth agape, eyes wide. Her bretata looked from Gerosa to her, then back up to the hut. Karliah followed, glancing up just as Amma shoved her captor over the railing. The man, unlike Gerosa, never got up from where he landed.

The deck was a blur of swinging limbs and weapons. Both Amma and Appa had escaped their bonds, but not the prison of the platform. Appa's arzok hung over the railing, her wings torn, her body contorted. Karliah couldn't see her head. Amma's came in for another attack, then another, until Amma shouted for him to flee. He made it a few feet away from the hut before one of the masked men's arrows took him down.

Karliah screamed as he flopped to the ground like a fallen leaf. She started for him, but Konar grabbed her arm and pulled her to him.

"We have to run," he said, yanking her along.

"But Amma and Appa," she blubbered. Snot and tears stained her lips, lacing her tongue with salt.

"They'd want us to run," Konar repeated.

Karliah allowed him to draw her into the shelter of the jungle, toward their sanctuary behind the falls. As they ran, she stole one last glance at their family hut, a place whose bittersweet memories would now be forever marred by that day's events, and all because of her, because she listened to that stupid voice telling her she knew what was best for the scroll, that Appa and Amma would waste it, that even Konar wouldn't do what was necessary. That deep down, it was meant to be hers and no one else's.

Appa and Amma were still alive when the hut disappeared from view, but that gave Karliah no solace. They were unarmed, outnumbered, and trapped.

And it was all her fault.

KONAR

K onar made them wait in the cave for two sunrises, slipping beneath the fall's curtain only once to retrieve pyanne from nearby trees. There was no reason to believe anyone would find them, vast as the jungle surrounding their hut was, but he didn't want to risk it.

At first, he'd feared Barky would lead the highborn to them, that Karliah may have slipped and told the old man of their favorite hiding place once upon a time, but when no one came the first day, that fear evaporated—alongside the hope that Amma and Appa had escaped, had fought their way free.

He never spoke his conclusions aloud. He didn't need to. Karliah's face told him she believed the same, and her soft whimpers at night told him she'd blame herself for a long time, if not forever.

It wasn't entirely her fault. Amma and Appa knew better than to risk everything. Barky knew better than to trade the closest thing he had to kin for a chance to live out the rest of his days in luxury. And Konar? He'd awakened the night Karliah stole away. Saw her put the herbs in Appa's pipe weed. Knew deep down what she was doing and could've, should've, followed her to confirm his suspicions. But he'd rolled over in his cot, faced the wall, and lied to himself that the situation would sort itself out, that he didn't need to exercise a false sense of control.

Never again.

KARLIAH

She'd never sail again.

Not that she'd ever liked it to begin with, not really, not the way Appa did, as much as she wanted to appease him, to be the smaller, womanly version of the great Brineheart. Out on the water, there was no wilderness to explore, no streets to get lost in. Just the tireless creaking of the ship as it rocked and the festering stink of ocean life. And now, the only reason she once loved it was gone, ripped from her and carried off to a foreign land to await what would likely be an unfair trial. Assuming they weren't dead already.

That's what Konar believed. She saw it in his listless face, in the way he slumped against the railing of the ship they'd secured passage on in exchange for Konar's skills as a deck boy and Karliah's knack for coaxing pity through wide, watery eyes. Resting but rarely sleeping. Eating just enough. Never letting a complaint slip from his mouth.

She had to believe it, though, that they still lived, that their journey to Az Zar and the entire abandonment of their lives on Zelos would be worth it. Her urge to rectify her mistake was too strong, her desire to see forgiveness and approval in her parents' eyes too overwhelming. Besides, she would've felt it, wouldn't she? If they were truly gone? That gutting, all-encompassing emptiness that clawed at her consciousness would've taken hold.

One more day, and they'd land. They'd sneak ashore, rescue Amma and Appa, and make everything right again. And if not, well...

She'd retrieve the scroll, and the world would burn.

KONAR

"**D**o you want to starve?" Konar said, shaking the stick-turned-skewer at Karliah. "I literally watched it die and fought a dog for its meat. It's cooked through; look."

Karliah recoiled from the outstretched skewer and shook her head. Her face curled into a scowl, so reminiscent of Amma's it sent a pang of longing resounding through Konar's chest.

"Uh-uh." She pushed it away with her finger. "Skirvin are poison, Konar. Literally. Have you seen their spines?"

Konar withheld the remark that, yes, he'd had to see the damn thing to butcher it for meat, hadn't he? Instead, he pulled a piece of the green tinged meat off the skewer and popped it into his mouth, careful to avoid breathing through his nose. Karliah studied him with a raised eyebrow as he swallowed the piece, quickly chasing it with another bite for good measure.

"I've seen other street dwellers eating them," he said, softer this time. "You can't live off them forever, but removing their spines removes the poison, and this one didn't look sick." When Karliah didn't appear convinced, he added, "At least eat enough to have strength for tomorrow. If everything goes as planned—"

"Fine." Karliah snatched the skewer, bit off a chunk, and swallowed it whole.

"First Amma," Konar muttered.

"What?" Karliah took one more bite, swallowed it whole as she had the last, and resumed pacing around their small fire. "Just eating enough to have strength for tomorrow."

Konar reluctantly finished the rest of the meat and kept his gaze on his setata all the while, only taking it off her when other street dwellers drew close enough to the flames to highlight the greed in their eyes.

He and Karliah had spent the past few days keeping to the secluded parts of Cadar's outermost district, disguised in thick, rough spun cloaks they'd pilfered from unsuspecting drunkards their first night in Az Zar's capital. They begged and worked for what scraps they could and stole or killed what they couldn't. The air was far colder than back in Zelos, and the people far ruder, but this only made the oversized cloaks easier to justify and their presence unsuspecting. And though their Zelosi look was not that of the locals, it wasn't rare enough to cause alarm. No one appeared to be searching for them, at least. The emperor and his ordained highborn likely didn't think a boy of twelve and a girl of eight capable of surviving in the jungle, let alone gaining passage to a foreign land where they plotted to free their convicted parents.

Someone coughed something thick and wet onto the stone path a few feet away from where Karliah paced, her breath making clouds in the air. When the figure lingered, then approached, Konar rose from where he reclined against a compost barrel and placed himself between the intruder and his setata. A moon slipped out from beneath the clouds, illuminating the intruder's hollow face.

Human. Sick. Old. Konar ticked off the major features and, registering none of them as a threat, took a step closer. The man coughed more bile onto the street as he limped away, cursing.

"You need to be more aware," Konar said once the man was out of earshot. "I know most of the street dwellers are harmless like him, but there are some far more capable, no doubt with malicious intent, and I..."

I might not be able to protect you. The truth waited just beneath the surface, like a seed ready to sprout. He kept it buried for another day.

"Bah." Karliah tilted her chin up to study the moons. "Who says I'm not? I heard that man hacking up his lungs far before we saw him. I'm not as incapable as you think, Bretata."

Konar squeezed her shoulder. "I know. I just can't imagine losing you, too."

"Don't worry." She playfully punched him, causing the oversized hood to slip off her head and reveal her nyrian white braids. "You're stuck with me forever." Then, with a furrowed brow, she added, "And Amma and Appa aren't lost. We're getting them back tomorrow. Making this all right. I bet they already have a plan to escape. Probably don't even need us." She laughed at this, though Konar sensed a forced nature about it.

"Probably."

As Konar retrieved more fuel from the compost barrel, wincing at the pungent odors that escaped when he removed the covering, Karliah asked, "Do you think they've been hurting them?" Her voice, which had taken on the nature of a far older woman's the past fortnight, slipped back into that of a young girl's.

Konar swallowed, cast some food scraps and straw onto the fire alongside a single rotting board he'd broken into smaller pieces. "Not enough to render them useless. They want them to talk, to give up the scroll or us."

"They don't need both of them for that." The sudden realization cropped off Karliah's words. She tucked her knees into her chest and rocked. "That man in the market yesterday, he said they've been starving them, probably torturing them, and, and—" She shook her head rapidly, rocking faster and faster until Konar wrapped his arms around her from behind.

"Breathe," he whispered into her ear. "Just breathe. That man didn't know what he was talking about. He probably wanted a good story to tell his friends, is all. Alright?"

Konar winced at his lie. The man had claimed to work at the island prison just off the coast of Cadar proper. Based on the descriptions he'd given of Amma and Appa, Konar had no reason to believe he'd lied, even if he had bloated the details a little to impress the gathering crowd.

It's about time those filthy Zelosi pirates pay for their corrupt ways, the jailor had bragged to all gathered in the center of the cart-laden marketplace. *They've seen to it the Brineheart will never walk again, and his awskada whore only has her hands to guide her sight.* When asked what their crimes were, he'd reclined on a bench, hands laced over his protruding belly, and said, *Existing,* to which the crowd roared laughter.

And in a way, the jailor was right.

Konar tried to shake the memory as they huddled in the space between the fire and the compost barrels, tucked in the heart of the alleys looping around Cadar's outermost district like tributaries. The wind nipped at his face, the coastal damp soaking through to his bones, but he hardly noticed. It was a small price to pay for a chance to start anew. If everything went as planned the next day, they'd follow their parents after the trial, cause a distraction, and help them escape in the vulnerable moment between city and island prison. It was risky and likely to go wrong, but what choice did they have?

"Karliah," Konar whispered as she nodded off to sleep, her head cradled in his lap. "Why did you take the scroll?"

She stirred, but didn't open her eyes. He'd never come outright and asked. The answer was clear enough to him: she'd not trusted their parents and felt it best to take matters into her own hands, as she often did. So clear that he only asked now to offer her a little more peace, to manipulate her response into something positive, to give her courage for the next day. To tell her it was alright, that he understood, may have even done the same had it gone on much longer.

He was not prepared for her answer.

"I wanted it," she said through a yawn. "I wanted it so badly."

Konar couldn't piece together a response before her light breathing gave way to gentle snores. As they lay nestled on the hard, cool ground of a strange city, surrounded by those who'd cause them harm, given the chance, Konar looked up at the moons and cursed himself for his curious mind and big mouth.

He'd find the scroll again, and when he did, he'd destroy it.

The sun did not shine the next day, leaving the sky awash in a gray pallor not unlike the complexion of the highborn who'd led the assault on their home a fortnight prior. Konar and Karliah awoke to a drizzle just before dawn, one that left their cloaks damp for the foreseeable future, probably until they could shed the layers on their voyage home.

Not home, Konar corrected himself. Not any longer. They'd go back to retrieve the scroll, of course, but anything beyond that would be a risk. Appa would want to sail west to Orillon, Amma would push for somewhere beyond that, beyond Neharem, maybe even as far as the Beridian Isles.

"Anywhere but there," he muttered under his breath as he stretched the morning stiffness out of his muscles.

Karliah gave him the look she usually reserved for beggars strewn out in alleyways, mouths agape and hands twitching as they pondered the revelations brought upon by sedare mushrooms. "What?"

"Never mind." He started down the alleyway, careful to dodge the freshly formed puddles of both rain and urine. "Let's hurry. We need to find a position near the front."

Neither of them spoke as they wended their way from the narrow alleyways of the outer districts to the larger and ornamented paths of the inner city. Scents transitioned from sea waste and excrement to the more pleasant aromas of sun-blood blossoms, spices, and grilled meats. The closer they drew to the courtyard located just outside the palace, the more congested the route grew. Konar doubted the emperor had made his pursuit and loss of the scroll public knowledge, which meant all the people elbowing around him were keen to watch the trial, and the likely negative outcome, of the pirates. The thought twisted his stomach. He quickened his pace, keeping one hand tight on Karliah's sleeve while the other drew his hood further down his face.

No one from the inner districts gave Konar and Karliah so much as a second glance as they melted in through the courtyard gates with the other servants, beggars, and plain folk. For every highborn wrapped neck to toe in flowing swaths of brightly colored silk, a dozen others slouched in roughly woven tunics or dresses and cloaks of neutral tones. The soldiers surrounding the perimeter made Konar a little queasy, but he dismissed it, convincing himself they had no reason to be searching for them, that it was merely their identity-masking uniforms that made them appear shifty.

Karliah gasped, and Konar followed her gaze to a set of stairs leading up to a marble platform, upon which sat an altar of pure nevethium. He'd only seen the crystals a few times in his life, and all those times put together didn't come close to the amount on display in the courtyard. Large Mavist banners hung down either side of the altar, and in front of it stood an ornately dressed nyrian with hair that ran all the way to the ground. A smaller, though no less lavishly dressed, version stood behind the man Konar assumed to be emperor, the specimen somewhere between his age and Karliah's. At least a dozen soldiers stood guard around the sovereigns, all brandishing spears with gleaming lyvium tips. Konar rose on his toes to search the crowd for any sign of Amma and Appa being ushered to the platform. He found none.

Karliah looked up at him, eyes wide and questioning. Before he found the words to comfort her, a loud, deep ringing sound echoed through the courtyard. It came from a giant instrument made of metal and shaped like a disc. Konar tried to recall its name. Appa had spoken of such an instrument after one of his visits to Cadar. A robed man holding a mallet struck the gong—yes, that was it—again, repeating the sound, then stepped back with his head bowed as a cluster of guards emerged from a curtain behind the altar. They dragged two figures and shoved another forward, leaving them collapsed in a pile at the front of the platform.

Konar withdrew his gaze to collect himself, guiding his attention to the cracking stone beneath his feet. A small sprig of green sprung through, and he found its presence oddly comforting. How brave for such a little plant to grow where it was unwelcome, to risk living despite its inevitable doom.

For a moment, the surrounding noise faded, blurring into the background, the figures growing muddy and distant. A lightness seized his mind. It was only when Karliah sucked in a sharp breath that he forced his attention back to the platform, back to what he didn't want to see or comprehend.

It wasn't Amma and Appa up there. Not really. Not anymore. The man's legs were contorted around him at weird angles, broken and bloody, bloated and bruised. His head had been shaved and his face was so swollen from beatings that it was beyond recognition. Only the arzok tattoo on his exposed arm gave him away. Dried blood covered the woman's face. She no longer had eyes or a nose. She sat there lifeless and silent, teetering slightly whenever the wind picked up. The last man was mostly intact, if not a little roughed up.

He wouldn't be for long. Konar's gut told him none of the pirates on display would leave the courtyard alive.

The emperor bellowed something about pirates not deserving a trial; how no one betrayed the empire and got away with it. Konar refused to process the words as they berated his ears, refused to watch what happened next. He drew Karliah's face into his chest and imagined Amma's singing as she stroked his back to help him fall asleep. Imagined Appa, frustrated but proud as he taught Konar to navigate with only the stars to guide them. Imagined all their meals around the table, all their sunsets at sea. All the bad was worth the good, every hug worth a million shouts. Every smile worth the moments of anger.

His throat constricted. He dug his fingernails into Karliah's back as the emperor shouted and the first blade fell.

As if capable of mercy, the rain began to fall harder, masking his tears.

Another shout. Another blade.

Karliah sobbed beneath him.

And the last.

Konar rubbed the snot from his nose and gave Karliah a jerk. "Come on," he whispered as the emperor made his closing remarks. "We have to go now."

Karliah followed him like a stray pup through the crowd. Others were already making to leave as well, helping to mask their early departure. They were almost to the courtyard gates when a boney finger shot out from the worn robe of a street dweller lingering beside their means of escape.

Konar's stomach dropped. The street dweller from the night prior.

He must've followed them, must've—

"Pirate filth," the man rasped in Zarith.

A buzzing sound filled Konar's ear as people glanced over at them, brows knit in suspicion. Karliah clung to his arm.

"Pirates," the street dweller cried again, this time a shout. "Pirates! Pirate filth! Zelosi scum!"

Konar bolted for the gates, Karliah in tow, but someone stuck out a foot and sent him careening to the ground. He bashed his chin on stone, looking up just as soldiers fell in around them.

"No," he stammered. "No, no, no."

Then they were grabbing at his hands, his legs, shoving spears and swords in his face, ripping his setata, the only thing he had left in the world, away from him. A hilt slammed into his skull, and when he woke again, he was no longer Konar Brune.

And never again would he be.

EPILOGUE

T he boy and the girl huddled together in the corner of the stables, nestled inside the now vacant stall of the mare who'd died earlier that day while foaling.

Twins had been her undoing. One perished some time prior to the labor and had caused a fatal infection in its mother. The other breathed fresh air for the better part of the morning before dying in the girl's arms as she hummed to it softly, so softly, the song of a mother's love. The boy looked on with a hollowness beyond his years. No moisture blurred his eyes.

Unnatural thing, twins in horses, the stable keep had said as he dragged the lifeless, still womb-crusted bodies of the foals away. As unnatural as children committing crimes at their parents' behest. He'd glared at the children as he spoke the last bit, then tossed them hardened bean cakes left untouched by the other servants. Though hard to chew, the cakes were of good quality, passed down from the palace inhabitants themselves, then to the palace servants before finally making their way out to those who tended the animals and gardens. Those not allowed indoors.

That didn't bother the boy and girl. Clean, sun-blood blossom kissed air was better than the heavy incense plaguing the palace. The slaves and servants assigned to the courtyard and its surrounding grounds were sincere, if unkind. And they both preferred being away from the watchful, judging gazes of the highborns, happy to serve creatures who regarded them with genuine appreciation in the form of velvety muzzles and gentle wickers.

Happy enough. Being hurled the occasional sneer-accompanying insults of *awskada spawn* and *pirate filth* was better than beatings. Better than death.

"It looked at me like it knew it was going to die," the girl said, speaking of the foal as she kicked at some of the dirty straw. The mare's blood still stained patches of the stall's bedding, but neither child had the vitality to do anything more than push it away with aching limbs. They'd get to it in the morning, along with thirty-nine other stalls, as was part of their duties.

The boy gingerly eased himself into a reclined position, using the forgotten birthing rags as a pillow. "It probably did." His body begged for sleep, but his mind rarely gave in to the request. Eventually, his eyelids would close.

But then the dreams came.

"It looked at me like Amma," the girl said in the disciplined voice she'd adopted since their arrival at the palace moons prior. The boy thought she sounded too old for her now nine years. The girl felt safe when she spoke that way, like a proper adult.

More grown up than most, she thought. Then, "Amma looked at peace, didn't she? In a way?"

No one without eyes can look at peace, was the boy's initial thought, though he didn't say it aloud. He rarely said things aloud anymore. "In a way," he muttered, shutting his eyes so she couldn't see the lie in them.

The girl snuggled up beside him, her back to his. A soft, irregular heaving rattled her small frame. The boy recognized the illness for what it was, but he allowed her to keep her dignity. Drawing attention to it was meaningless, anyhow. He couldn't offer the comfort she sought.

The night air was cool, enough to remind one of mortality without making the act of outdoor sleep insufferable. Mounts in the stalls over huffed from time to time, the only sound to break up the otherwise eerie quiet, and the sweet musk of grains and manure were only partially tainted by the metallic taste of congealed blood.

As sleep began to vie for the boy's consciousness, the girl sat up and touched his shoulder with gentle but intentional fingers.

"This isn't the end," she whispered.

The boy's eyes shot open. He pressed up on his elbow and regarded the girl's wild, violet eyes. A shiver rippled down his spine as he realized he no longer knew the girl within.

And, perhaps she no longer recognized him.

"Not for Amma and Appa's legacy," she continued, "and not for us. No one knows where it is but me, and—"

The boy clapped a hand over the girl's mouth, his own eyes now wild enough to rival hers. "Hush, foolish girl, for those who shouldn't hear will be the ones that do." He cringed as he said it, hating how he sounded like the worst parts of both of his parents, the parts he didn't care to remember. As a peace offering, he removed a bit of straw that had tangled itself inside one of the girl's braids. "Do you mean to avenge them?" he whispered in a barely audible voice.

She glared at his reprimand but went on, more out of eagerness to finish speaking her thoughts than acceptance of his exercised authority. "They can never be avenged. No lives can be taken that would equal what we've lost."

No contradiction came from the boy's lips. He urged her to go on by meeting her gaze, giving her hand a tight squeeze.

"But we can still make it right," she said finally.

"It?" the boy pressed.

"Everything." She stared through him as she unraveled the endless possibilities in her mind, each one better than the last. "Our lives, other lives. Quinaria. Even all of Quorath. We'll make everything the way it should be." For a moment, she came back to him. Captured his gaze with her own. "The way Amma and Appa wanted."

The stable door creaked open. Both children jumped up at once, peering over the stall door to the thin shaft of light cast by the moonbeams. They held their breath and each other's hand. A shadow passed back and forth over the light, then stopped just outside the door for what seemed an eternity to both children. The girl's nails dug into the boy's palm as the door groaned open further, then—

A small cat slunk into the stable, making its way to the rafters with a few dexterous leaps.

They both giggled, then collapsed back into the straw with breathy sighs.

"They wanted it kept hidden," the boy said after they settled. He kept his voice low. Next time, it might not be a cat. "They said it wasn't to be trusted."

"No." The girl shook her head in an abrupt, childlike way. "They said it wasn't to be trusted with *other* people. Not you. Not me." Small fists balled up at her sides. "We were meant to have it, Bretata. Can you not see it? Why else would it have been entrusted to you?"

The boy had no logical rebuttal to this and crossed his arms in response.

"The spirit walker gave it to *you*," the girl repeated, not bothering to mask her irritation. Her tone made the boy smile, for it reminded him of his amma. "No one else before, and who knows how many others had tried. How can you still doubt yourself?"

A hundred reasons swirled around in the boy's head, but they'd all be lost on his setata with her mind made up just so.

And even though he didn't possess her conviction, her certainty, even though he highly doubted the odds of their survival in pursuing escape, let alone keeping the scroll safe, he couldn't tell her no. Couldn't be the last one to let her down. The one to snuff out what remained of her impenetrable, childlike hope.

"I don't doubt you, Karliah, so I'll try not to doubt your faith in me." He pulled her in close and stroked her hair, trying to forever capture the moment, refusing to even acknowledge the possibility that anything could be powerful enough to come between them.

"Promise?" she whispered, holding her pinky finger out.

He intertwined his pinky in hers. "Promise."

They huddled together, their bodies providing enough heat to withstand the cold, their love providing enough courage to withstand the hard days to come.

"And promise one more thing," she murmured as her eyelids began to close, her fingers wrapped tightly around her only remaining possession: a tiny doll with beaded, violet eyes and hair of bleached leather. The first gift her amma had given her, and the last thing tethering her to the life that once was.

The boy was half asleep as well when he replied. "Anything."

"Promise we'll always be together. You and me against the world, but never each other."

"Never each other," he whispered back. "Just us against the world."

And in that moment, they both meant it.

AUTHOR'S NOTE

Thank you for reading *From the Depths*. I hope it provided you an escape while giving you some thought-provoking moments to dwell on. If you can spare a few minutes, I'd be ever so honored if you left a review on Goodreads and on Amazon (or wherever you purchased the book from). Aside from purchasing a book, leaving a rating and review is one of the best ways to support an author. Your feedback is important to me and will help other readers both find the book and decide whether to read it.

If you'd like to stay up to date on my writing journey, upcoming releases, and be the first to receive exciting news, please sign up for my newsletter at bshgarcia.com/subscribe. When you sign up, you'll also receive exclusive access to a **free** prequel novelette, *From the Ashes*. Set over two thousand years prior to the events in *Of Thieves and Shadows* (volume one in *The Heart of Quinaria*), this story follows Igtheos and Elize amid the Nyzarian civil war and the deadly Siege of Cadar.

Note: if you're having difficulties navigating to the subscribe link via your e-reader, it may be easiest to just type the website into your phone or computer. Not all of the e-reader browsers are up to date.

You can also interact with me on Instagram and Twitter (@bshgarcia), and follow me for important updates on Facebook, Goodreads, and Threads (same handle).

Finally, I'd like to note that the fictional lands of Quinaria are inspired by events and legends from all over the world. None is intended as a faithful representation of any one country or culture at any point in history.

Thank you again for your support. I can't wait to thrust you into the next installment of this epic saga.

-Bethany Sharon Herold Garcia

THE RACES OF QUINARIA

Beridians {bur-rid-ee-in}

- Physical features: Feline-esque beings covered in fur instead of skin with the tails and ears of great cats, they stand six to eight feet tall and walk upright

- Lifespan: Average of 300 years

- Traits: Poisonous claws, nocturnal vision

- Location: Predominately their isles with the exception of a few backhanders and explorers

Humans

- Physical features: Standard human variations

- Lifespan: Average of 75 years

- Traits: Skilled with tools and weapons

- Location: Some in eastern Az Zar and Neharem, but Orillon consists predominantly of humans

Myrem {meer-rem} (*also classified as Vysilliam in some be-lief systems, one of the three original races comprising a trinity of beings suited for sky, water, and land*)

- Physical features: Unknown, but rumored to be am-phibious

- Lifespan: Rumored to be 1000 years

- Traits: The ability to breathe underwater

- Location: Unknown as they've not surfaced in genera-tions

Nazrath {naz-wrath}

- Physical features: Giants rumored to have been three times the size of a nyrian while still resembling their basic features

- Lifespan: Unknown

- Traits: Immense strength and intelligence

- Location: Once northern Az Zar, but rumored to have retreated to the Uncharted North where they died off

Nymans {nigh-men}

- Physical features: These rarely conceived human–nyri-an hybrids tend to result in dual to tri-toned skin, hair, and eyes while retaining the nyrian pointed ears and luminescent eyes

- Lifespan: Average of 200 years

- Traits: While they tend to carry the superior health

and intellect of the nyrian parent, most nymans struggle with infertility

- Location: Neharem and Orillon

Nyrians {neer-ree-in} *(also classified as Vysilliam in some belief systems, one of the three original races comprising a trinity of beings suited for sky, water, and land)*
- Physical features: Slightly taller than humans on average, white hair, pointed ears, and luminescent eyes

- Lifespan: Average of 500 years

- Traits: Strong immune systems, superior intelligence (due in part to the extended lifespan), better vision

- Location: Az Zar, Neharem (rarely found in Orillon)

Shaktar {shack-tar} *(also classified as Vysilliam in some belief systems, one of the three original races comprising a trinity of beings suited for sky, water, and land)*
- Physical features: Unknown, but legend says they could fly

- Lifespan: Rumored to have been eternal

- Traits: Unknown

- Location: Unknown, but legend says they occupy caverns in eastern Orillon

Skulmor {skull-mor}
- Physical features: Canine-esque beings covered in fur

instead of skin with the tails and ears of wolves, they are roughly eight feet tall and prefer to move on all fours (though they can walk upright)

- Lifespan: Average of 40 years

- Traits: Hulking strength and powerful fangs

- Location: The Skulmor territory (nomadic)

GLOSSARY

–please note this glossary incorporates all terms intro-duced in The Heart of Quinaria series to date, therefore it may include terms not present in this installment–

abdano {ahb-dah-no}- a Zelosi dish comprised of wild hog and pyanne.

Agaas {uh-gaas}- the capital of Neharem.

amma {ah-ma}- Zelosi word for "mother."

anderberries- a sweet and salty berry that grows in the forest near the Apáasutai coastline. Commonly used in baking and for wines.

appa {ah-pa}- Zelosi word for "father."

arkthanax {arc-thuh-nax}- an Az Zarian invention capable of performing the work of a hundred men, much faster, and with little to no breaks. Production includes textile weaving, mining, etc.

arzok {ar-zock}- a nocturnal, flying mammal with sizeable fangs and forelimbs adapted as wings. Native to Zelos.

aspar {as-per}- the basic monetary unit of Az Zar, also commonly used in Orillon. Made from lyvium (see definition) and cast into coins of varying size and shape to denote value.

awskada {aw-ska-duh}- the Zelosi word for a person, most often a woman, who professes or is supposed to practice magic or sorcery. Also used in Az Zar.

backhander- someone for hire, usually for dangerous and/or illegitimate work, such as brute force, smuggling, bodyguarding, assassinating, etc.

belzaith {bell-zay-uth}- the Hispen word for "underworld spirit." Also, the name of Grokhion's ax.

Beridian Moonlight- a strong, sweet, fortified wine made from a rare fruit and a potent plant native to the Beridian Isles. It is highly alcoholic yet surprisingly palatable, and the secret plant added during fermentation creates a unique high for the consumer. (Also just called Moonlight).

blue fever- a disease caused by nutrition deficiencies and characterized by swollen, bleeding gums, raging fevers, and the opening of previously healed wounds. Common to pirates and seafarers.

Bongaiyo {bong-eye-oh}- believed by many cultures to be the mother of all stormbirds; also a constellation used for navigation made up of ten stars that form the rudimentary shape of a stormbird. Contains the south star, Elonias.

bretata {bray-tah-ta}- Zelosi word for "brother."

bugana {boo-gah-nuh}- a fibrous, stalky plant sacred to the Zelosi people. It is often harvested for its sugar and used in cooking or distilled into kolaash. Its stalks can also be dried out and hardened for building materials and tableware.

Cadar {cay-dar}- the capital of Az Zar.

Caman {cay-men}- immortal beings loyal to Mavet. Depending on one's belief system, they are said to be angels, demons, or myth.

Chai'Tik {shy-teek}– a goddess of great power, she is revered, demonized, or considered farce, depending on one's belief syste m. Also called The Daughter.

deathdrop– a carnivorous plant that lures bugs and small birds to it by posing as if it has dew, when the little orbs are, in fact, sticky and poisonous. Native to Zelos.

deathstalker– giant insects equipped with stingers that release a deadly venom. One of the three orders of The Great Beasts of Old.

Dzro Jiazin {zhro-jye-zin}– (also called The Cleansing) an Az Zarian holiday celebrating the foundation of Az Zar.

dzvadra {zhvah-dra}– the Zarith word for "deathstalker."

edoja {ee-doh-juh}– the Nyrinian word for "father."

Elonias {ee-lon-eye-uhs}– the south star, part of the Bongaiyo constellation.

endei {en-dye}– an Apáasutai word for "a bad omen."

Eskos {ess-kohs}– the smallest island of Zelos.

eudna {yood-nuh}– the Zarith word for "father."

eumma {yuum-muh}– the Zarith word for "mother."

Everworld– an eternal paradise that is key to the belief system of some tribes and peoples.

Feasting Moons– summer. Contains the months Gryphar, sub-Gryphar, and Phoenal.

Gathering Moons– fall. Contains the months sub-Phoenal, Mavalar, and sub-Mavalar.

gidmörni tree {gid-meeorn-ee}– a species of tree that grows on the cliffs of the western Neharem coastline and produces rare blossoms that provide extreme clarity when consumed.

Great Beasts of Old– the first of the beasts, wise as the Vysilliam (see definition) and blessed with long life and special abilities. Includes stormbirds, seaserpents, and deathstalkers.

groundshakes– a sudden and violent shaking of the ground, sometimes causing great destruction, as a result of movements within the land's crust or volcanic action.

gwanei {gwah-nay}– small, bipedal, carnivorous reptiles that travel in packs of thirty to fifty, using their razor beaks and toothed tongues to take down larger prey. Native to Zelos.

hal-eudna {haal-yood-nuh}– the Zarith word for "grandfather."

Haeshol {hay-sholl}– a torturous, eternal holding place that is key to the belief system of some tribes and peoples.

helgin {hell-gin}– a monstrous boar with four tusks.

highborn– a term used to describe persons belonging to Az Zar's elite class.

Hispen {hiss-pen}– the official language of The Beridian Isles.

hoksanu {hoke-saw-noo}– an ancient Neharem tradition allowing one to challenge a chief or the high chieftain for the right to lead. It consists of two to three trials between the leader and the challenger.

Khiev-Tatamic {khey-ev-ta-tah-mec}– the first god, the creator or discoverer of the world, he is revered, demonized, or considered farce based on the belief system of the character.

kinawa {key-naw-wah}– a stout, aromatic, erect annual herb native to Neharem. When smoked, its leaves release a psychoactive substance. It's believed to have therapeutic properties and enlighten one's mind.

kolaash {koh-lah-sh}– an alcoholic liquor distilled from bugana and sweetened with pyanne.

kuba {koob-uh}– a nutrient-dense grain native to Az Zar. It has a nutty aroma and is most often steamed.

kuza {koo-zuh}– private military used by the great houses in Orillon.

lightbursts– contraptions that light up the sky with bursts of greenish-yellow light for celebrations. Commonly found in Az Zar and Orillon.

living trees– giant trees found in northwestern Neharem. The citizens of Agaas live in them, and they are nurtured by large nevethium (see definition) crystals referred to as "hearts."

love-giver– a person who engages in sexual activity for payment. Commonly found in Orillon and considered an honorable profession, unlike the whores of Az Zar who are often slaves.

lyda {lye-duh}– the Nyrinian word for "demon."

lyvium {lye-vee-um}– native to Az Zar, it is stronger than any other metal, yet light and flexible, making it ideal for weapons.

Mavet {mah-vet}– a god of great power, he is revered, demonized, or considered farce, depending on one's belief system. Also called The Son.

Mavism {mah-viz-um}– the official religion of Az Zar, it contains rigid practices surrounding penance and the giving of one's self to Mavet, the savior, and the government.

mizol {mye-zoll}– a crustacean that produces a fluorescent, waterproof ink.

moon cycle– roughly a month's time on Quorath.

Munskahan {moon-ska-haan}– the capital of Orillon.

Myremese {meer-rem-eez}– a lost language once spoken by the myrem and retained by a handful of scholars.

nazrath– giants descended of the nyrian bloodline.

nevethium {nuh-veth-ee-um}– radiant green crystals whose absence, when overharvested and misused, renders the surrounding land inhospitable. Also referred to as "the heart of Quinaria."

Novitae {no-vee-tay}– a Neharem holiday celebrating the story of creation.

Nyrinian {nee-rin-ee-in}- the ancient tongue once spoken by all nyrians is the official language of Agaas. It is also spoken by upper-class citizens in Az Zar who choose to honor the ancient ways.

nytak {nigh-tack}- a deer-like creature native to Neharem with scaled hooves and a long, furry tail.

pocoaon tree {poh-co-uhn}- a tree species found throughout Quinaria in generally cool areas. Most grow near rivers, lakes, or swamps, and have limber, dangling branches.

populum {pop-yoo-lum}- a hallucination-inducing root native to Orillon.

Prophets, the- a sacred order coinciding with Az Zar's foundation. They studied the natural world, kept records, explored alternate histories, and some believe they learned the powers of gods.

Prophets' Scrolls, the- parchments containing years of research, history, and philosophy, penned by the Prophets. Rumored to contain magic spells unlocking the power of gods.

pyanne {pigh-ann}- an acidic fruit with sugary and spicy notes, used in both sweet and savory cooking. Native to Zelos.

Quinaria {quee-narr-ee-uh}- the central landmass on which the story unfolds. Includes Neharem, Az Zar, and Orillon. See map for details.

Quorath {cor-rath}- the planet in which Quinaria resides. Includes all of the known and unknown world.

ravager bird {rav-uh-jer}- a carrion bird species with brilliant red feathers, found throughout Quinaria.

Resting Moons- winter. Contains the months Onelar, sub-Onelar, Vynar, and sub-Vynar.

rujpati {roozh-pah-tee}- Az Zarian appointed government officials of Zelosi provinces.

ryptan {rip-tin}- a large avian-reptilian hybrid with feathers and scales. They rely on large talons and fangs to hunt and defend. Native to Neharem.

sandcat- large felines with long fangs. Native to Az Zar.

seahawk- birds that are both aerial and aquatic.

seaserpent- giant serpents that live in the sea. One of the three orders of The Great Beasts of Old.

sedare {suh-dare}- a mushroom native to Az Zar and known for its medicinal properties, specifically pain relief.

seers {see-ers}- a contraption worn over the eyes to enhance poor eyesight.

setata {say-tah-ta}- Zelosi word for "sister."

Shaktari {shack-tar-ee}- a lost language once spoken by the shaktar and retained by a handful of scholars.

shieum {shee-um}- new weapons made of lyvium and nevethium that launch far deadlier projectiles than arrows and make a booming sound when used. (Also called thunder-makers).

siren- a nocturnal bird known for its eerily human/nyrian sounding music and its shimmering midnight blue feathers. Native to Zelos, but also found on the islands inhabited by the Yustano people.

skirvin {sker-vin}- large, vicious rodents with poisonous, sharp spines and impeccable hearing. Native to Az Zar and commonly found in large cities like Cadar and Or Zahal where they can burrow under homes, in tunnels, and crypts.

sleepstalk- a root native to Zelos that can induce sleep or render one unconscious. Too much can result in a painless death.

snatcher- a thief.

Sowing Moons- spring. Contains the months Chailar, sub-Chailar, Tiknal, and sub-Tiknal.

spirit walkers– angels or demons, or lesser gods and goddesses, depending on one's belief system.

starflies– Zelosi word for a winged, soft-bodied beetle with luminescent organs.

stormbird– giant birds of prey capable of manipulating/channeling the weather. One of the three orders of The Great Beasts of Old.

Stormrider– an individual who has bonded with a stormbird and gained the privilege of approaching it, maintaining physical and emotional contact, and riding on its back.

sun-blood tree– a species of tree found in Az Zar that produces small, tangy citrus fruits. They have vibrant crimson blossoms and are found in much of Az Zar's architecture and general imagery.

terredon {tehr-eh-dawn}– a flowering plant whose rhizome is widely used as a spice. Native to Zelos and Az Zar.

toi {toy}– a fermented plant drink with fruity undertones common among the southern tribes of Neharem.

Tongura {tahn-goo-ruh}– the largest village on the main island of Zelos.

tulek bear {too-lek}– giant bears of the north.

tungata root {toon-gah-tuh}– an earthy root located in northern Neharem that is often ground up into a powder and put in teas for energy.

tuross {ter-ross}– flying lizards bred from ancient times when messages needed to transcend water, land, and sky. They are still a primary form of long-distance communication.

Vysilliam {vye-sill-ee-um}– believed by some to be the three original races of Quinaria comprising a trinity of beings suited for sky, water, and land. Includes the shaktar, myrem, and nyrians.

watcher– someone who helps patrol or guard in Neharem.

water dancer- a short-lived, slender insect with delicate, transparent wings and two or three long filaments on the tail.

Westmun {west-mun}- the official language of Orillon.

yasaaka {yuh-sah-kuh}- a small paddle boat/board used by Zelosi locals to fish and for easy travel around and between islands.

zaka-zaka {zah-kuh-zah-kuh}- a large marsupial serving as the primary form of transportation in Orillon deserts.

Zarith {zare-rith}- the official language of Az Zar.

Zelos {zell-ohs}- a collection of islands off the southwestern coast of Az Zar.

Zelosi {zell-oh-see}- referring to the various peoples inhabiting, and dialects spoken on, the islands of Zelos.

zidel tree {zai-dell}- a tree with an angular crown and erratic branches with large, fanned leaves. Its bark is often consumed or smoked for its clarity benefits and general feel-good sensations. Found in Zelos and southern Az Zar.

ACKNOWLEDGEMENTS

I wrote this story while procrastinating on another book in this series, so thank you, my bad habits. Thank you more specifically to Konar and Karliah, for making me realize I needed to do some deep diving into your past to better understand your present.

In terms of real people, I owe the most thanks to the husbean, Jared. From plot lines to Pinterest boards, you've given a wealth of time and energy to Quinaria, and I can never repay you for that.

Oh, wait. I made you co-founder of Lost Relic Publishing. We're even. But thank you for feeding me non-dairy Ben & Jerry's while I type. And for coming up with the initial cover design for both novellas.

Fine. You're irreplaceable.

To my critique partner, Kaylea, thank you. You are instrumental in my craft now, and I think I would feel naked if I didn't have you to look over my work in its earliest stages. Your feedback is always spot-on, and your care genuine. Thank you.

Kelsbot, I think you're actually my biggest fan. I swear you believe in my stories more than me, and you don't know how many times you've kept me going when I've wanted to quit. I owe you at least thirty-seven more lake days to make up for this. Thank you.

To my editor, Jon, and my proofreader, Dom, your names rhyme, and that's just fun for me on a superficial level. But seriously, I wouldn't be turning out such polished products without you, so thank you for your professionalism and attention to detail. Please never leave me because I hate searching for new editors.

Thanks to the team at MIBL for putting together another eye-catching cover. You've worked hard to capture the essence of Jared's designs and make the novellas fit with the main series installments. Your talent shows.

My beta readers Kaela, Lisa, Tim, and Andy helped me see this story with fresh eyes when I'd maxed out my capability to make it better. Thank you for taking the time to read an unedited manuscript to offer your feedback and help me hone the story I wanted to tell. Thank you all so much.

Special thanks to Lindsey for marketing my books better on Instagram than I do. You are a champion of indie books, and we love you for it.

Björn and Éowyn, you two are simultaneously the most inspiring and distracting people in my life. And though you make it take ten times longer for me to draft and publish, I don't think I'd be doing this if it wasn't for you both. Thanks for letting me be your mom and write at least two minutes a day.

Saké, Piña, Mimi: you're assholes, the lot of you. Top-notch snuggles, though. 10/10 heckin' good pupper and meows.

Thank you to everyone still along for this journey through Quinaria. I'm honored by every single read and review. There's so much more to come, and I can't wait to drag you through Haeshol and back.

Until next time.

May your sunrises always hold promise, and may your sunsets always hold peace.

ABOUT THE AUTHOR

B. S. H. Garcia is the author of the epic fantasy series, *The Heart of Quinaria*. A household manager by day, writer by night, she graduated with honors from The University of Colorado with a bachelor's degree in English Writing. To get into character for her stories, she trudges through the woods in cosplay with a mead-filled drinking horn and has traveled from Oregon to New Zealand seeking inspiration. Visit her online at www. bshgarcia.com. There, you can get your hands on a FREE copy of *The Heart of Quinaria* prequel novelette, *From the Ashes*. All she asks for in exchange is your soul.